Matt Hill was born in 1984 and grew up in Tameside, Greater Manchester. After completing a journalism degree at Cardiff University, he trained as a copywriter. Matt currently lives and works in London. You'll find him on Twitter @matthewhill.

THE FOLDED MAN

Matt Hill

SANDSTONEPRESS
HIGHLAND | SCOTLAND

First published in Great Britain by
Sandstone Press Ltd
PO Box 5725
One High Street
Dingwall
Ross-shire
IV15 9WJ
Scotland.

www.sandstonepress.com

The Folded Man was placed runner-up in the
2012 Dundee International Book Prize

The publisher acknowledges subsidy from Creative Scotland
towards publication of this volume.

ISBN: 978-1-908737-34-2
ISBNe: 978-1-908737-35-9

Cover design by Graham Thew, Dublin.
Typeset by Iolaire Typesetting, Newtonmore.
Printed and bound by Totem, Poland.

For Dom.

Acknowledgements

Love and thanks to family, near and far, here and not. Especially my grandparents, Julia and Alan, and my brother, Alex, for their stories; and my godmother Val, who told me to never apologise for being honest.

Thank you to those who read drafts and chatted through ideas: Gareth and Sarah Hulmes, Gareth Clarke, Edd Barber, Cat Gee, Mike Williams, Ed Vanstone, Chrissy Hoey, Gemma Kirkpatrick, Amy Hoyle, Chris White, Heather Taylor, Nick Moran, James Leadley, and Mark Griffiths – as well as Anna Day and everyone involved with the Dundee Prize. To Caroline and Gary Smailes, the kind of gratitude a rainforest's worth of greetings cards couldn't say.

Many thanks to my agent, Sam Copeland, for his belief and his graft – and to Eilidh Smith at Sandstone Press for all of hers.

And then to Suzanne. Without whom –

0.

Brian means to divide himself by two.

He wants a thick lamp post for starters. A long enough road for seconds. And in the boot, there's enough cable to string up an ox.

So when he finds the right post on the right road, he rigs it good. He ties it off with good strong knots. And when he's set, he leans out the car window and hooks the cable's other end with a stick. He pulls it into the car and runs a lasso round his waist. There, by his crotch, he makes the same knots again, strong despite himself, grazing sweaty palms on cold steel.

He winds the window up. He remembers some facts from a dirty yellow post-it:

I am a special kind of bastard. Fat and grim and dying. A challenging kind of bastard, too. Didn't know it? Skin an apple and you might miss a worm in the middle.

In the rear-view mirror, the Pennines. Through the sunroof, slate. Forward, a sign pointing into Manchester, half a mile ahead.

Course, you aren't meant to tell, he writes on a fresh sheet. You're meant to show.

Brian sets off hard. Chasing some kind of happy-ever-after.

On the pavement, the cable uncoils – a long, sharp snake in school-jumper grey.

1.

Thursdays, Diane comes round to spoil Brian's day.

Brian, he's fannying about in the lounge with a tin between his legs, watching his CCTV monitor, watching her walk up the drive, through rain, through the door. Into the hallway, watching her shake her brolly up the wallpaper.

Brian! she shouts, bright as buttons. You in?

Through here.

Diane clumps through the hall and wanders in. Looks around and wonders.

Brian sits in his chair – the wheelchair in the middle of his world. Today it's the tin, but she knows from here that all days are the same. All days, every hour – that he's trapped. A fat man entering a cold middle age with nothing left to burn. A fat child, a chubby little boy, ageing without grace. And all these things: smoking and eating and sleeping between these damp, bare walls. Sitting under bare bulbs, through the power cuts and water shortages; the riots and the radicals at his door. Always in this same chair at the arse-end of Manchester, capital of the north.

Their cold city, the blinking city. That's our Brian. This man without hope or humility.

Brian mixes goop in his old paint tin, turning circles with the back of a wooden spoon. No mistake: the room stinks – really stinks. Stinks of all sorts. A low-hung smell

2

of washing-up liquid and something worse. It catches in her throat the way chilli powder does; a burnt smell, like dust over heater filaments.

Morning, she says. It's a smooth, even voice. For a moment she thinks she sees her breath.

Washing's by the stairs, Brian says. Didn't get round to it.

Diane smiles. Diane looks at all the sand on the floor. She tells him not to fuss. Diane says, You're a funny onion.

Brian goes on stirring tight circles in the goop. His eyes hardly move, dry and red at the edges.

Still waters run deep, Diane thinks. Another northern loner on the list in her pocket.

What's that you're making there then? Diane asks. She unbuttons her bright red coat and slips it off. She pats down her dress.

Exfoliant.

She nods again. Smiles that weapons-grade smile.

And you've done your exercises this week?

Few dips, aye.

You'll never get out the bath one day, she says.

He looks right through her. I'll buy a crane.

Still wearing that hat inside, too, Diane says. Do your skin no good, will it?

Well, he doesn't like her dress either. Too bright, isn't it. Something for the bees.

No ironing, love? Brought your week's food as well. Autocooker of yours still on the blink I'll bet, but I've chucked a few meat cartridges in there anyway.

Brian's wheelchair creaks.

Dial ham you get tuna, he says. Dial tuna you get steam. Dial lamb you get scolded. So yes. And my cigarette papers?

3

All in the bag. Oh, and no eggs available anywhere close this week – or that's what they're saying – but the milk'll last you.

He looks at the CCTV monitor again. White fuzz and fizz, passing cars, bushes growing every which way but straight. An old, purple Transit across the road – that sometime symbol of hard work. A workhorse turned weapon in riot-time. Pigs, they called them round this way. Ironic or wit or whatever.

Back to Diane, back to her red file.

Them kids been back? Diane says.

He looks at the monitors as if to double-check.

Not this week, Brian says. Bastards need sending the Wilbers' way.

Can't wish that on anyone, love. You must call the police first.

Brian smiles into the tin.

Got a pen then, treacle?

He points at the sideboard. A pot next to the Bibles and Torahs, the books and post-its; the empty crisp packets and the tacky porcelain. Next to relics of the olden days. His older ways.

Diane stands to fetch it.

Sign here then love, she says, tapping a dotted line on the paper. She's bending over him and holding the paper close. Brian can see her bra, the crease of her breast. Everything's red.

Just so's they know I've been, she says.

Brian writes his name while Diane takes the washing through. The washing plus the shopping bags. He's written Brian with his surname while she drops all the bags on the cold lino. He hears her rumbling about in the cupboards. Looking for detergent he basically doesn't have. For storage space he doesn't need. He hears her put the

4

shopping away. The washing machine door shutting. The click. The pump and the water –

Next Thursday then, Diane says, back now and putting her coat on. Diane who never flinches, never blushes. And you best take care.

Brian puts the tin down and stops mixing. Pulls out the creamy wooden spoon and puts it flat on the plastic bag that's spilling sand by his side. He lights the black end of half a joint and rolls the tip round the glass ashtray.

I'm dying, Diane, he says, as she opens the door to leave.

Diane stops and turns.

You big wally, she says. All of us always are. But listen, son. You must stop cooking your hair.

Two men load Brian onto the community care bus. It'd be a kind of comedy in another setting, this man being folded up and tinned by the able. His weight makes him awkward to shift up the access ramp, and the wheels of his chair keep jamming alternately, swinging what pass for his feet from left to right.

Your transport company, it says up the side.

The bus, it shows its age now: an armoured half-track carrier the council converted to run supplies, and long since sold off to the city's health trust. Inside it's oil and pop rivets, old sandwich wrappers under seats, old stains and burns on the fabric – like nothing about public transport changes, or nothing ever will. Only this thing has six-inch portholes where the old buses had plate glass. And it's a slow cooker. An iron lung, pushing stale air through hollow men.

The men shepherd Brian straight up the bus, rolling him backwards. He clings to his blanket and looks down while death-grey eyes scan him from all sides. The men

5

don't speak as they strap his chair to the subframe. From here, there's only rain ahead. The smell of diesel. The heads lolling around on slack necks and sloping shoulders.

To his right, in a single corner seat, a boy is masturbating under his coat.

Brian asks him to stop – a quiet word if anything. Really, you wouldn't hear it over the cries and the gibbering. Wouldn't notice for all these recitals and prayers.

The boy stops all right. The boy's face splits into laughter. He makes the effort to lean over and spit a fat greenie in Brian's lap.

Mong, the boy says. Bloody paedo. Fuck off with you.

Brian falters. The bus takes off, grunting forwards. Brian turns away, wipes the slime off himself. He closes his eyes. Shuts them so tight; buttons them shut against the world.

Brian, he worries the bus might roll on a corner. Wishes it weren't a single driver responsible for all these people. He imagines himself crushed, split, burnt. His chair on fire. He's scared of fallibility is why: the one bad habit they always excuse.

Only it's 2018. Trust is a currency now.

The wheels on the bus go round and round. And Brian's bones are jumbled all the way into Manchester.

In Argos, the city-centre branch, Brian blocks the queue. He knows it, too, but pretends he doesn't. Pretends like he hasn't noticed everyone. It's an aloofness the wheelchair affords; an arrogance that goes unchallenged.

He's looking at watches – classic watches with faux leather straps, edged in gold, the kind that really say something about a man. They're four pounds each, every one. A clearance sale. A closing-down sale. That's how

6

come they're by the exit. Right next to the shattered windows. End of days for another dead chain.

Brian pores and ponders and pushes fingerprints over glass. Shakes and listens to each watch in turn.

Brian likes that every watch measures time differently. A second out, others an hour slow. A better way to look at things.

In the face of every watch, the queue threads past behind him.

Brian retches bile in the disabled toilet at Burger King.

Brian holds the hand rail tight. He's got half a Chicken Royale down his beard and front, and mayonnaise on his hat. He starts to wipe himself with a handful of low-grade tissue, pulling thick bunches off the reel to wipe Fanta and sticky chip salt from the back of his neck, thinking this is what wheelchairs get a man.

He pulls his hat off and pushes it into the low sink for disabled people. He watches a faint trickle of hot water running over it, beading in places on loose strands of wool.

Bastards, he's saying. Dirty little bastards.

So Brian cleans his beard in the water; splashes his face for good measure. The tissue tears and smears and sticks in his whiskers. His eyes are watering he's so wound up.

Under the striplights in the Burger King disabled toilet, Brian's head looks like a buttered chessboard. That's because he keeps his hair the way farmers do their fields. Like crop rotation, he tells Diane on Thursdays, or anyone else who'll listen. How a man gets more one side when the other's shorn close. As rapeseed, as wheat, as hair.

To manage it, he's measured his head into quadrants and divided each of these by length. Shorn. Short. Long.

7

Longer. With a comb, he's divided each of these quarters into many little squares of hair, and greased every bit with Vaseline for freshness. Every piece, every point, is sectioned off with an old rubber band. It makes for slick, wet squares, right the way across. The hat keeps it neat; a crown to fasten it close.

Every morning, he cuts out a tail of hair and cooks it with breakfast.

Oftentimes, the community bus is late back.

Gone eleven, Brian runs the bath downstairs. He takes the paint tin of exfoliant, a box of salt and an ashtray into the damp bathroom with him. He left the skimmer in there last time. Good. He runs the tap, a trickle first, turning heavy as the boiler shrieks.

He shakes the salt and pours it. He makes the sea.

When the water's on the right side of hot, Brian undresses. He does it slowly, awkwardly, mindful of old scabs. He peels himself. The aches of a long day out are racking his spine.

From his chair, Brian clambers into the bath lift harness – pausing for breath, shuffling for comfort – before lowering himself into the tepid water. Into the stinging water. Settling, easing, ready, he lights another three-skin joint and pulls hard, holding smoke down till his lungs burn. As he exhales, he takes a handful of exfoliant and begins to scrub away at the scales. He works coarse skin from his waist to his feet, drawing blood in semi-circles.

There's a rush, always a rush, that comes with this routine. Running sharpened hands over fused shins and fused calves and fused knees – the release and relief of finding the smooth beneath. It's the guilt and the hate, the pleasure and the shame. Sharp hands running over a single ankle, across the conjoined, flattened feet. It's the gritty sand he feels between his backside and the canvas of the bath lift. The salted water biting. The salt burning hot, ruthless.

On these powdered rocks, the mermaid throne. A throne in his six-foot sea.

He reaches for the skimmer, begins to fish bits of himself from the surface.

For Brian, in the bath downstairs and bleeding, the pink water holds a charge – an alternating current he's found for free.

2.

Early hours Friday, Brian's stoned and lonesome and not going to bed – a six-deck of lager in his guts with some down his top – and ranting down the blower to Mel at The Cat Flap.

Only Mel at The Cat Flap doesn't want to know.

Listen love, it's not that they mind seeing you, she's saying, over and over, tired and absent or halfway dead, but they're not coming round there again. No, not even in a pair. Not after last time. Hobby's over with this place unless you pay up front and pay more. None of your tricks neither.

Last time, he's saying back. What about last time? What even about last time. I'll pay for their donkey. Won't take twenty now will it? It's late. No patrols at this hour. Know a few lads with curfew licences anyway. It's safe, our road.

So come in and see us instead, Mel is saying, getting frustrated. Come here and have the choice. Cassie does scenes with anyone, ninety for half-hour. Door's open all –

Den of slags, he goes, interrupting. Hive of bloody wretches.

Mel from The Cat Flap sighs and hangs up.

Brian throws the phone at the wall.

Brian turns on the monitors, fuming and breathing hard. Dark out – too dark for the sensors – so he flips the night vision and starts to skin up another jay. Not tired now. Not sleeping soon. That damn purple Trans... outside. Not any neighbour he knows.

Brian leans back, blows smoke at the ce... and resentment. He's frustrated and he

Half a man, he says out loud to nobody, on his crotch, stick-man shadows thrown l

He pulls on the joint till his lips burn hot.

Half a man with itches to scratch.

Friday proper, the doorbell and the tannoy system wake him to spilled ashtrays and bad smells.

A visitor, sir, the tannoy says.

A new day. Another day. The same old day.

Morning has come with beer cans and brown chunks down his front. Spilled tobacco, smashed glasses and raw, sore skin. New scabs and old scars. Bile tickling his throat. There's a slender figure on the monitors and dry come in his hand.

Brian rubs his eyes. He scratches his thighs. His broken, stinging skin. He looks closer at the screen and sees a girl. He pulls his hat over his hair, clears his throat with the sour dregs of a beer. He wheels across to the intercom, ready for a battle.

I'm not in, he says.

The girl presses the doorbell again.

I'm not in, he says. Bugger off.

She turns and looks up at the camera dome. He can hear her through all the speakers in the lounge – can hear the echo on the relays upstairs.

A moment of your time, sir, she says. For the better good.

So Brian is ready for war. He buzzes the locks and wheels himself into the porch, arms cold and aching. The floor never seemed so old.

11

He opens the door. Some virtuous prick with a clipboard. Young, big teeth. A tight top groaning with promise.

Morning, she goes. I'm not here to sell God.

Bit of a shame, Brian says. I'm still after one of those.

Just want to ask you a few questions, she says, scanning the peeling wallpaper, the stripy rubber marks running over lino from door to door. If you've a few moments spare.

Not interested in sales, he says. On enough bastard databases aren't I? No brass to buy owt with, anyway. He rubs his hands together, then points at the purple Transit. That your van by there?

She shakes her head, glancing up and down and away, trying her hardest to ignore the shapes under his blanket.

Anyway, sir, won't keep you, she goes. I mean I suppose you, like all your other neighbours, love animals?

Brian pauses. Bites the tip of his finger, as though he's thinking. Then he says, Hate them. The neighbours too. Spies and liars, the lot of them.

She wilts, edges back, her smile gone.

He nods. That's right. Now clear off.

Daytime telly is soldiers and loansharks – soldiers and loansharks and heavy static since the reception gets worse every week. The soldiers are relentless, and getting younger with every tour. Fighting, surviving. Sleeping and waking and fighting some more. Out there, all together in the longest war.

Brian, he looks on through the fuzz – squinting and slowly smoking his last eighth in four long joints he made to last the day. Squinting and watching life filtered through head-cams on His Majesty's soldiers. Images of mortar tubes loaded, gunships landing, tracer fire lasering clouds. The waits through long government adverts about interest rates.

An age of celebrity caved to these anonymous heroes, these faceless villains. But really, Brian watches his country's endless war for love between the dead and dying. For hipflasks of hope passed round between the bombed.

It's funny: Brian doesn't remember where he was for the big things. The death of so-and-so, the bombing of here and there. Not like you're meant to. Not with dates and times. He can't ever say, if anybody asks. And actually, he only remembers the events of his own life through association. The personal events; the icons that scaffold a person's identity. Defining memories only remembered through the fixtures of everyday living.

So for Brian, he remembers the pattern of the curtains he was looking at when he took the call about his mother. The song on the radio when the first satellite fell, burning a streak over the Atlantic. The bubblebath turned flat by soap when they announced the very first curfew.

By nine evening there's a textbook sky, that rare thing, the colour of a thousand happy endings. Manchester blinks into life in the distance, suddenly more than sagging towers held up by billboards, entire buildings wrapped in holo-vinyls, lighting rigs you can still see clearly from eight miles out. The lights you can see from every approach; from the hills around; from the moors; from the roads that all point inwards.

Greater Manchester, he gets to thinking, looking out on his city. Fifty miles square, half a mile tall, five years dead.

And Brian, with a beer to open and a joint on the bounce, looking at those towers, thinks about new chances and new contracts. The ideas made at the top of them; the strategies okayed in boardrooms higher up. He gets to thinking about coke, so much coke, and then the girls. The brass.

How none of it comes down from those towers – just flits between.

At ten they switch on the city pillar – the Beetham memorial light. Brian watches the light flung tall. Their way to spear the moon. Their way to say sorry –

It's hard to know what we're remembering, Brian says, talking to the broken men on his telly.

Brian's out of weed and can't find the phone, forgetting it bounced or that he threw it to start with. He cuts a trail through card and forks, through smashed glass and fag dimps, to the hall and the foot of his stairs.

Brian hoists himself onto the stairlift platform, presses the right arrow for up. He looks at the stripes his tyres have left in the hall. The lift squeals. The chains grip, move. Brian climbs slowly over clean red carpets. Never used.

At the top of the stairs, he unstraps himself. He eases into his second wheelchair and turns a sharp right. Up the landing and into his archives.

His archives are the only thing he's ever built. Collected and stored and arranged by theme, they take up the lower half of almost every wall upstairs – shelves and drawers, dressers and baskets. Books, papers, trinkets. Posters, propaganda, beer mats. Notes from the DHSS, old cheques from birthday cards he forgot to cash, council replies to complaint letters – complaints about the reduced Metrolink running times, the state of the pavements. Photos of departed icons: the Big Bang, the Hacienda, the Cornerhouse. Photocopies he's made of receipts and of favourite pages from books at the library, before the library burnt. A pot of fifty-pence pieces he keeps for emergencies.

Dead skin in tupperware boxes. Nail clippings and elastic bands in another.

It's Brian's narrow, useless history of a time they lost – the golden years they never knew they had.

And Brian stops by the Olympic banner – five faded rings pulling him six years back. Before the riots and the radicals. Before the sharpline walls and all those lost wages. Before things rusted and the machines went bust. Before these decrepit vehicles salvaged to barely work in this functioning hell.

He picks up the phone by the bed he never sleeps in. N for Noah, he says into the mouthpiece – old buddy, old pal. He hears the click and the connection.

He notes the hesitation.

Hullo, comes a voice.

Avon calling, says Brian.

Meredith, you grubby old bastard! laughs Noah. How are you?

You know me, Brian says. Squaring circles.

And which service does Brian require? says Noah.

Usual.

Noah laughs again. I can be there in twenty. You're coming for a drive.

Noah talks the same old, same old, all the way up the hill to Werneth – old conquests and old wives, his terrible retirement and how he went about getting himself unretired. This rare, clear weather. How the rain will be home in the morning.

How he hasn't done too badly for some teenage graffiti artist turned freelance tagger by an ability to climb and aim a paint can. His old agent, Harry. All the fun they had.

That cheeky bastard wanted to pay five grand, Noah's telling Brian.

Well, I says to him, I go, Harry, you cheeky frigging bastard, I don't go south for less than fifteen. Not without a cannon and a cloak-suit. Send a man lone-wolf, past Brum – on the bastard plod no less – and you pay danger money for your troubles. Only he wasn't having that, Bri, and I could swear he laughed at me. He says, My clients don't pay danger money, our kid. So I says well you don't get our kid then. Bald twat.

Brian nods away. Owing to the weed, he's content to listen.

But every cloud, Brian, says Noah. This other time – and stop me if you've heard this – he's got me doing radio paint for a Sheffield agency, right? Like a proper job, this – archways and walls you colour in and turn on later. So there I am, dangling from ropes and suckers and earning our dinner, stencilling big names in big letters like always, and this bird with perfect tits walks under me – doesn't look up, doesn't notice. And I mean, they are perfect. Perfect. So I think fast and drip some drops of this rad-paint on her hair and down her back, a perfect shot. And I'm thinking, when they turn on this artwork tonight, love, I'll be seeing you around.

At the top of the hill, the peak of Werneth Low, Noah stops his dying old car. They look through dirty windows – the neon-lit city scattered before them.

So skin up, son, says Noah, rubbing his hands. Been too long.

The pair of them look out to the bright concrete. The grey city burning up with lights. Getting noisy down there, no doubt. Soldiers in the streets – the home guard tipped from their barracks. Dancers and hookers, the pushers, the pills, the poppers.

And in the centre, the brightest and whitest of all, the Deansgate memorial column goes up and up and up.

Just look at that beautiful sodding torch, Noah says to Brian, who's already rolling cardboard into a roach. Still gets me now to think of it falling. Funny how we hated it the first month it were up. And those tropical bastards who brought it down . . . Still. You remember that ad I pulled off, don't you fella?

Brian nods, concentrating on his build. This is what they always talk about on Werneth Low; this hill over-looking the slate basin.

Of course Brian remembers that ad.

The best, the best. Still the best, Noah says. The Beetham top panel, by me, your Noah – Captain Advertising, Captain Visibility. Mind you, I don't even remember the client's name now. Nobody would. But Brian, those tits! That big panel spread, those big tits and that grin; the tallest tits for miles! That were me, Brian – me and only me. Me on my tod with a vac-pack and no chalk. Me, gliding up them greasy window panels, looking in at all the call farms and laughing. Me, in the papers, me on the front page instead of our lads on the front.

And them fucking bastards came and took it all from me, Brian. Took my dreams with their backpacks.

Brian nods, lights the joint.

Council ever starts poking the sky again, I'll be up there, up there fast to say up yours to all of them, under black skies, hot sun, come rain or shine –

Brian nods, knocks the burning paper off the joint.

To say it were me and my lads who put this city in lights and large fonts and colours, hung its finest pictures, made Manchester proud –

17

Brian nods, inhaling.

To say it were me and my lads who did the dirty work and the deadly work besides –

Brian nods, blowing smoke.

Because you stand tall in this new world, young sparrow, even if this new world sits back and takes aim.

Brian nods. Passes the joint. Says, Do us a favour and drop me at The Cat Flap on the way back.

So Noah drops Brian in the old Asda car park round the corner. Less hassle that way. Plus it's not strictly a supermarket anymore, more a derelict warehouse for riot tanks.

Now don't be getting mugged off in there, goes Noah to Brian. You know these girls like to giggle and they like to gang up.

Been before, says Brian. Then he winks. Only the once or twice.

Still not a white face in there I'll expect, says Noah.

Odds that make? Brian says.

Not many, Noah replies. Some people have no trust for our darker sisters, is all. But still, if that Mel's still on the door I'd put one in the bank for her pal. Kind of woman you take time with, kid. Peel her open. Model material, or could've been. Sticky pages at the very least.

Brian grunts.

But anyway, listen, goes Noah, stepping out to help Brian into his chair on the passenger side. Come round the shop tomorrow. Crack of sparrows if you can. Something I want to tell you about.

Brian shrugs, yawns quietly. Nowt else to do, he says.

No, really, goes Noah.

Brian hops his wheels up the kerb, wheels his chair up on to the weed-split pavement, over dandelions poking tall through cracks. Over this redeveloped land that seems so given to nostalgia. Brian rolls forward, towards his fortunes.

Behind, Noah shouts: And catch a donkey home later – a proper taxi like these council bastards used to run!

Brian rolls into a dirty building with boarded windows; rolls into another kind of waiting room for another kind of medicine. A room where everything is wood panel and chipboard seats; where time has slipped and left its holes.

This is Brian – stolen away between dirty walls on dirtier streets, in and among the filthy girls and the nervous, waiting men – the night-time hiding them all. This is The Cat Flap – a bad rumour lit in purple by black-light UV bulbs, decorated with taxi firm numbers and takeaway menus. A promise of a better night out. Where yogic young women pout and spread themselves open on every wall.

Brian, nose full of beak, guts full with adrenaline, hands full of government cash. Brian, at the desk, where you pay with more than money.

Mel looks at his head poking up over the counter. She looks battle-weary, a fringe greased over one eyebrow. Old mascara, fresh red lipstick.

Cassie is it? she says.

Cassie and another, Brian says.

Would you like to see the menu?

He shakes his head. He feels sick and excited and ashamed. I'm just watching, he says. Just want to watch.

Well go and sit over there, Mel says.

He nods and pulls backwards; turns and pivots. Parks himself by a big man with violent tattoos of dead flowers and smashed vases. Shot birds flail down his arms in spirals towards his elbows.

19

Fuck you looking at, spacker? the tattooed man says.

Eyes to the ground. To the sides. Everywhere but.

Eyes to the videos.

Brian sees a man with four girls on a screen above Mel's desk. He watches skin pulled and spread and pinched. Watches girls slapped and spat on. Backsides spread and hairy hands spreading.

A small bell rings – a corner shop's door chime. Six girls walk out, begin to parade and twirl – a pageant inverted. In a line, they wiggle hips and push their breasts together. They push out their tongues and lick their bright white teeth.

Pink bikinis, spotted knickers, undersized bra cups. Long fingernails over gussets. They are numbered with lipstick on their bellies. One, two, three, four, five, six.

The tattooed man stands up and storms from The Cat Flap. Another fucking place filled with sand-niggers, he sneers, to Mel, to Brian, to the girls.

Numb, nobody really bats an eyelid.

Oi, goes Mel. Cassie's waiting.

Brian browses. Brian window-shops. Brian umms and ahhs.

Brian decides he likes the girl with the tattoo – a set of paw-prints that run from hip to navel. He wonders how many fingers have walked that path across her stomach, and whether that was the point. She is number four. She's just this side of five-foot-five. Tall enough for anyone by any standard.

A perfect height for Brian.

Number four has dark hair. Downy cheeks. Fuzz on her belly –

This one, he points, the vomit crawling to his mouth, his eyes starting to water. Number four.

She doesn't smile. Doesn't pout, doesn't anything.

He imagines trying to work out where he ends and she begins.

Cassie! shouts Mel, their manager. His host for the evening.

Cassie comes to the door, hair up. She has creamy skin and bruised shoulders.

You and Celeste, Mel says. She nods to number four and then to Brian. And this gentleman.

Brian knows they don't even pretend here. No Jacuzzis, saunas or steam rooms. No lockers for work trousers; nice massages for hard workers.

Cassie recognises him. She kind of pauses, then winks. She says to Celeste, you'll do a good scene with me, won't you love? Ninety for starters is it? Oh, he'll pay more. She grins at the room. At her girls. Girls one to six.

I think this one likes to watch. Don't you love?

And all the girls are looking at Brian. All the girls are giggling and ganging up.

In the room, on the bed, Celeste and Cassie kiss awkwardly. Brian watches, a metre away, at the foot of the bed. They've wheeled him in and wobbled their hips. They took his hat and ignored his hair.

The girls kiss some more. The girls undo each other's bras. The girls remove each other's stockings. The girls kiss each other's nipples. The girls writhe and stroke and slap. The girls push fingers into each other. The girls pretend to come.

The girls stop.

The girls talk in their mothers' language. In Urdu. The girls giggle and look sidelong at Brian.

Celeste pushes her round brown breasts in Brian's face. The fuzz against his chest. Cassie pulls at his blanket, exposes his hand, pulls at his joggers and his

21

underpants. All that polyester and precome.

Together, holding his arms back, they pull his hard penis loose. They spit on it. Cassie runs behind and pushes the chair to the bed, holding Brian's hands tight behind his head.

Celeste kneels forward onto all fours, her backside dangling from the edge of the bed, her hands pulling herself open. Cassie pushes Brian closer in his chair, howling with laughter. She bends and spits on him again. Bends and puts him in her mouth. A condom now, as if from nowhere, tight at the base, trapping hairs. But Brian's gone limp.

Brian goes weak.

The girls giggle some more. The girls, they pull Brian's joggers off.

The girls scream to high bloody heaven, covering themselves.

This is sex. Between grubby walls and dirty sheets. Between the bookies and the bus home.

This is sex. That bad, bad rumour.

The taxi driver's called Tariq. He finds Brian sprawled on the road, wheelchair tipped on its side, blanket torn. He finds Brian half-conscious and muttering, sick down his face, his hat hanging off his head. Brian who looks surprised and shocked and angry and lost. Who's all wet and tired and seems confused.

Tariq heaves Brian up, rights the wrongs. Big lad, Tariq is. Thick round the top half. He says, Good night, was it pal?

Brian murmurs.

Get you home shall we?

Tariq drives an old Vauxhall with a big boot and a heavy foot. Like most things in their city, it only works to

22

a point. Inside, the windows steam up quickly. Brian feels baffled. Numb by the arse. He looks out to low cloud and back to worn seat fabric. Draws three stickmen, two legs apiece, on the windows. Then, he rubs them out.

Fact is, there aren't many Asians with curfew licences, so Brian's surprised to meet Tariq. It's rarer still that he's gone unchecked by the local lads. They strung a guy from a lamp post the month before – called the police and said we don't pay fares to their type. But he doesn't ask. Doesn't care. This is getting home. This is going to bed.

The taxi stops at the house. Tariq looks out at the sharp-line fence, the cameras, the floodlamps, the wrought-iron gates.

Tariq passes him a business card. I'm around and about. Could do with some more regulars.

Brian takes the card. Grunts. Looks out at the purple Transit, parked on his side of the road.

The house where Brian rots.

3.

Saturday. First light is a fresh yolk dashed across the Pennines – an orange line that turns the edges of morning pink. But there's always fragility to sunshine over the moors – a pregnancy. Because for everyone here, everyone nearby, warm weather on these hills is just weather waiting to relapse.

Brian is falling through the morning – falling and burning through. He's been drinking and smoking since four. By seven, he's still numb but somehow focused, scratching hard from toe to hip, trying harder to roll a thin joint for later. At eight, he calls for a cab and waits in his porch, locking and unlocking and relocking the deadbolts.

Brian smells of burnt hair and yesterday's clothes. He hasn't noticed the sick on his coat sleeves, and definitely hasn't clocked the bent spokes on the left wheel.

The taxi runs hot, running reds. You don't stop on this road. Not for porn shops or bookies; the gold exchange or the social clubs. Not by the boarded-up terraces with their lights still on inside. Not for the fresh flowers on railings; not for the wet red sand beneath them. Not even for some kid's body in a shattered bus stop, head spread over a metre in long red ribbons. The party from the night before.

By Noah's shop, Ancoats, bordering town, Brian pays

for the cab. Another ten pounds to cross about ten minutes of hell. The driver says nothing; he just gets out, opens the boot, and unfolds the wheelchair.

Brian shuffles himself across the backseat.

A shoe shop was never the most imaginative front, but Noah's drugs factory is getting so close to legit he's taken to handing out business cards with his bribes. There's isn't a bastard missing on his books – pigs through pimps, councils through ex-cons. He's the go-to man. The shop's just there so he isn't rubbing important noses in his success. A kind of upright hobby to hide the plants and the pills.

Brian rolls through puddles and up kerbs. He clips the doorframe, clatters the entry bell.

In one aisle, Noah's holding a pair of school shoes to a little girl's feet. Her mother is thumbing some catalogue, licking fingers, pulling corners. Brian recognises her. It's the young woman who knocked on about donations and animals.

Very early, pal, Noah says, not looking up. Having a bad do this morning – mind waiting?

The little girl stares at Brian, at the hat and the beard, the clothes, the blanket. The woman turns, smiles thinly, not really noticing, not really listening.

Brian shakes his head, holds up his baccy tin. I'll be outside.

Don't be a bloody hero, says Noah. He winks and points downstairs.

In the service lift with concertina doors, the whole thing wobbling and scraping down the shaft. At the bunker's edge next – inches of concrete-reinforced steel with an old bank vault door. Keying in the password – the codes, the capital letters. Eighteen characters plus the eye-scan. All that trust.

Hissing doors. Spinning locks. Hydraulics or pneumatics or something else besides.

Into the paradise factory. Into Noah's war room, the dark engine beneath his shop. A hole where fat walls make hiding places for powerful men.

Rolling in, his eyes adjusting, Brian hears the burbling hydroponics, scans the tools put down on busy work benches by the projects and the prototypes. In one corner, a bank of manual pill presses. Another, a rack of antique swords. In the centre, two bookshelves, each filled with car manuals and engineering theory. A shelf for pseudo-science. A shelf for UFO literature, truther literature. A shelf for battle tactics. A shelf for DIY transistor radios.

The switchbox hums. The lights flicker.

Brian rolls around the room, a slow pinball buzzing between Noah's interests and inventions. There are blueprints here – blueprints and plans. There are home-made grenades, too. Fertiliser drums and jam jars filled with industrial fasteners. A bin of clothes – all camo – some urban, some not. A weights' bench. A climbing wall. Gas masks. Space on the wall for reclaimed flags and symbols turned out by relatives after wars they never talked about. Something bad, pointy, under a lot of old bedsheets.

All of that in this world, this lair, where Noah plans some kind of new Manchester.

So I get this call, Noah says, giving Brian a start. Shit, pal. Make you jump there?

Don't sneak up like that, Brian says.

Noah walks over, smile as big as garage doors, a proud man in his dark bunker.

26

Brian, he goes, almost too close. I won't take long. Just let me tell you about this call.

Brian says, Okay.

Noah lights up and grabs a seat. So an old client of mine – did some big campaigns for him before the riots. A few afterwards. Garland he's called. Biggest name I've handled, come to that. Guns, chems, 'lectrics – he's in all the main sectors, or anyway the main sectors left. Heard of him, right?

Brian nods.

Big boys then and big boys now, and no bastard mistake. One of the few private contractors the state even touches, actually. More call farms than a suit's got stitches. More capital than sensible places to put it.

Right, Brian says. And what's he want?

Well he calls me up first thing. Just before you, come to that. He says, Noah. Noah, my man. You may remember me. Done us a good spread way back when, a full-colour holo-vinyl on the Arndale tower. Piddler now, isn't it, he says – a tiny pecker next to the Ferguson – but you got us results.

So I say to him, Hello Mr Garland, all polite – polite since it's not often you speak to clients so direct. A nice change from Harry taking a cut anyway. So yes, I say, I say, I do remember that job Mr Garland. I say, I was younger then, of course; more balls than brains. But I recall the cash was decent, the fanny was mint and the rep from a Garland job was priceless.

So Garland goes, Well, son. I'm interested in using your services again.

Noah winks at Brian, smiling again –

And I mean I'm thinking, Bingo! I'm thinking last time I worked for this guy, I could go to ground for a while. Another job like that, I'm living like a king again. Spending cash like some tower-level dick.

Brian nods.

So what did he want you to do?

Say again?

What's it all about?

Well, cut a short story shorter, fella wants me to attend a tech convention on his behalf. Take a few notes on his up and coming competitors while I'm at it. It's up in the hills, up our way. Exclusive as owt you've heard of. And no, I know – normally you call on me to climb things fast, put adverts on buildings faster. But then again, I'm thinking, what the fuck. I'm that go-to guy. It's cash. I'm out of retirement. This guy Garland trusts me to keep quiet. Thinks I'm a requirement.

So you're doing it? says Brian.

Lad's paying me to get over to a tradeshow, Brian. To spy for him. Course I'm bloody doing it.

And you brought me here to tell me that?

No, says Noah. He stands up and kneels by Brian's chair.

Brought you here because when a man takes a short cut, a man gets muddy feet. Because I reckon I'm taking you with me. 'Cause if I take you, I won't have to climb walls, look through top windows. No short cuts. No muddy feet. Noah taps his head. Got brains, see. Better brains than that. I can walk straight in there with my pal Brian in his wheelchair; my pal Brian who I care about deeply. My pal Brian, a local war vet – Brian who lost a leg doing heroic things in far-away lands. My pal Brian, who's filthy rich on charity profits and wants to walk again. They deal in mobile war tech, son. They'll have walkers, robotics, platforms there. And you'll be there in your Sunday best. You'll be there with your medals. You'll be interested in their products – and they just might be interested in you.

28

PR opportunities. Photo opportunities. Development opportunities. And me, I'll be taking notes for our man behind the curtain.

Brian doesn't know. Brian feels angry. Lost in Noah's bunker.

These are places and meetings where real men go to sort out futures, says Noah. Not these hippy bastards working on AIDS drugs for people we won't ever meet. Cancer pills for old bags we'll never see or sleep with. These are the men who design real aid for real people. For me and you. For our country. Aid for heartbreak. Aid for the lost or losing. You hear whispers – good whispers –

Suffocated, sobering, shaking.

Men like Garland are men who want our country back, says Noah. These are the men to bring long wars home. No more Beetham towers. No more lads with exploding backpacks in our museums and post offices. Competition's good. Healthy. He wants new ideas from the best in his sector. From a couple of blokes in particular.

So why isn't he going himself? Brian says. If they're after the same and all?

Noah shrugs. Noah sniffs.

I don't know, he says. Complex thing, this military-industrial complex. Can't ever say for definite, can you. But they don't like our Government much, these lads – doubt they're keen on Garland's connections. Think Garland sold out or something. Purists aren't they. Sometimes you forget how business is business.

Won't folk there recognise you?

Noah scratches his neck. Fingers his palms. Stretches a bit.

Don't know, he says. Maybe. Probably. What's to say nobody there bloody invited me?

Brian shakes his head.

It's just you've gone from scaling windows to rolling in with me.

Noah strokes his chin.

I'll have a shave or something. Don't fret the details.

And what do I get for helping? Brian asks, scanning the bunker. What if I don't want to come?

You will. It's something to do, says Noah. And after, well. Goes well you'll get as much minge as you want paying for. Classy types – European types. I can arrange that –

Trapped between walls and under ceilings.

Noah stands and sits on his weights bench. Noah spreads his legs and leans back.

So what thinks our Brian? he asks.

Brian looks on. Brian has a dry mouth.

I don't know either, he says.

On the weights bench, Noah starts pulling twenties.

Brian watches the brackets of vein expand down Noah's skinny biceps. The tendons on his neck pop out and in. Brian thinks of a sky gone pewter, with drizzle falling to dampen their day. He listens to Noah breathing through sets, twenty reps, twenty-five reps. Watches him plant hands on the floor, sixty incline push-ups, another round, then up into handstands and a short hop to his climbing wall. No chalk, just up and across, around and about.

Just think of all that fanny you could enjoy, Noah says, breathless.

When is it? goes Brian, following Noah across the wall.

Tomorrow night, says Noah, panting now, a crescent of sweat under each armpit. Best keeping your kind on their toes.

Brian says nothing, thinking, shite, and so soon. He

waits, rushing, hating himself and Noah's presumption, wanting a line –

Wanting out of a world he's running the edge of.

Later. Still Saturday. Under blankets, in his chair, Brian the night-owl sits and thinks. Brian is smoking and drinking and scratching hard in bursts. The same three things he's done since twelve-noon. Same three things for five long years. His day measured in the scabs and skin he keeps for the archives.

Brian is scared to sleep. Frightened of the dreams –

He looks out at the Beetham memorial; the centre of Manchester's gravity. A lustrous sunset, only turned on its side.

Brian thinks to run a bath; to dig out the salt and a pan scourer besides. To eat something. To trim the hairs of a quadrant on his head; reapply his Vaseline and his elastic bands.

Brian, he's thinking hard. Long and hard – about what-ifs and consequences. About slag and pavements. Torn between blackmail and bribery; between duty and finances and morals. Between chances and lies. Torn because he might not even care. Because it's about using Noah. Using Noah or feeling used.

Brian, he's weighing addictions – addictions, vices, sins. Easy money. Dirty money. Smoking and drinking, watching and waiting. Trusting and breathing. A decision to make. A favour to call in later. A promise to keep. A stooge. A vet. A liar. A bastard. Always that bastard. And now this chance for hips fused to steel.

Maybe he's thinking too much. Might even be fun, he tells himself. Leastways of interest.

And all that war tech. Mobile war tech, maybe.

PR opportunities and more.

Opportunities like making a half-man whole.

31

4.

Sunday, early doors, Noah takes Brian to see a man about a suit.

They travel fast from east Manchester to south – to Didsbury, a fortress suburb hanging a few miles beneath the city centre. There are barricades to cross and papers to show. Old-guard gents waving shotguns at check-points – waving them through with two-hour permits and winks that double as warnings. They're given a transponder. They're told to leave it on the dash – a box with eyes to watch, ears to listen. There'll be no riff-raff here – not in Didsbury.

Brian and Noah pass handsome gardens and clean pavements. Round this way, there aren't potholes or exposed mains to slalom. The people of Didsbury power their own land with generators; their cars with fuel they make from used cooking oil. They recycle the way the whole city used to. Their kids still play outside – wash working cars for neighbours, run the community paper-rounds. People walk dogs. Men work. Men wake to alarm clocks and warm, willing wives.

Didsbury is a time-capsule. Didsbury, strung at the edges with sharpline, is a suburb running on tradition.

Brian and Noah don't talk. Brian and Noah drive slowly.

They pull up on double-yellows outside a Victorian semi. Noah says, Alight here for quality tailoring by Manchester's finest. Next, that reseating routine, the last three minutes of any journey forever the same. Noah gets out and opens the boot, unfolds the wheelchair. Brian shuffles. Opens the door. From seated to sitting. To rattling and rolling.

Noah rings the bell since Brian can't reach. They look thick as thieves, the pair of them. Lumps spooned from the same gravy.

The door swings. Inside, inside, says a small, white-haired man, the look of a jeweller about him. A busy-body. A small man with big pockets.

The suit maker's house is foppish, regency in style. It's almost a parody of things that used to matter – pointless; a way to speak of class when nobody's left to care. Boots and brothel-creepers all over the place. Dozens of nude mannequins: totems of strange alabaster muscle staring ahead. Two or three wearing ties.

They enter the lounge. Smell pipe smoke and see old paintings – paintings of hunts and gentry.

The suit maker, he bumbles and bimbles; flits between the furniture. It's obvious he works in measurements and time. It's true what Noah said, too – true that the suit maker asks his visitors few questions for good reason. When the needy visit Didsbury, their hours here are tallied, their movements carefully logged. The needy can be dangerous, and too many answers from dangerous people can fill your brain; can make you an asset.

How long do you have? is one question the suit maker asks.

Hour and a half tops, Noah says, checking his watch.

Not long enough, the suit maker says. Your friend is rather substantial.

Long enough to get something off the shelf, Noah says.

It's a rare thing in Didsbury, is rudeness, says the suit maker. A rare thing.

Brian looks down at his blanket; at the tube of meat he calls a tail. He says, I'll only need a jacket. Extra large or whatever. A white, ironed shirt to fit.

Well, we may have something in storage, says the suit maker. But as I say. It may be difficult. Arms up, please.

Brian raises his arms, feels the tape measure tighten; the tape measure wrapping his chest.

Very good, says the suit maker. He disappears down a narrow corridor.

Noah turns to Brian. You'll look a bobby-dazzler, kid.

But Brian feels trapped between this handsome wallpaper and his duty.

The suit maker returns with two jackets. He walks like a sad pigeon, his belt tight and scaffolding his belly.

A suit jacket to broaden the shadow, the suit maker says, holding up a pin-stripe navy jacket. Or this smart number: a jacket to sharpen the shoulders.

They help Brian put the first jacket on, shuffling the collar. It crushes his chest. The suit maker and Noah are smiling thinly. Brian looks back at himself, all sharp lines and deep creases. A crushed flower.

A suit to broaden the shadow. A suit to sharpen the shoulders.

They help Brian try the second jacket. It's a convenient fit.

Expect we'll need to taper these parts, says the suit maker, pulling at the material on Brian's flanks.

Brian doesn't feel himself at all.

No time for that, says Noah. We'll pay up and move on.

Move on where? says Brian.

Noah looks at Brian's hat. See a man about a haircut.

In the car, leaving Didsbury with the suit jacket over the back seat, Brian's eyes are wet and watering. Brian doesn't want to see any man about any kind of haircut. Brian can't look at Noah. Can't really see for tears. Cannot speak for these deepening fears.

Noah is shouting. Noah's taken Brian's hat and pulled a sun visor down. Noah's saying, Look at yourself, man. Just bloody look at yourself. You think that's credible? Think that's what an old soldier looks like?

Brian is sobbing, Brian can't look in mirrors, can't understand. Don't do this to me, he's saying.

But Noah is shouting and swearing, isn't he. Driving faster. You fuck this up for me I'll swing for you, he shouts, hurling them at sixty towards this hair appointment in the centre of town. Balls this up and we'll have ourselves a big fall out.

Brian has a plastic bag filled with hair. He is quiet. He is numb. He is Samson, shorn bald. Medusa, beheaded. King Nisos, bereft.

The bag of hair's in his lap. Something lost he must preserve.

Noah starts the car.

All right. Good lad. Now, we go yours first, he says. Got the medals in the boot. We get ready there –

Brian feels scared and cold. No longer comforted by a myth he's made; no longer protected by the strange habits of superstition.

I don't want you at mine, he says.

For now, till the stubble grows out, he's been forced from a habit formed on the back of his mother's words.

Formed on a belief system fuelled by encyclopaedias and legends; ancient tales of boats led to rocks where sailors drown.

35

Rocks where survivors eat the flesh of sirens – kill and eat the harlots who brought them so close to death.

Eat them and live forever.

Another stop, this one for petrol and limp butties. Two men from the margins at the old Texaco on the edge of town. Right on the edge of all things light and everything good – the dusk yards they call it round this way. The dusk yards being a line you cross to find yourself tipped into night and all things worse. Tipped beyond the city – where roads are blacker without neon and street-lamps. No curfews. No law.

Brian stays in the car on account of his tail; stays in the car to cut another pair of lines for them both, to straighten his tie and smooth his collar.

Want owt? says Noah.

Nah, says Brian, playing with the baggie.

Brian hears Noah fill up the car. Smells petrol, breathes it down. Brian pours the coke and starts to smooth the lines. Sees Noah by the pay-grate, stacking up tight in a queue three-long. Sees the shotgun pointed outwards.

Brian edges the lines. Cuts them. Edges them again. He looks up at the splitting canopy, across at the empty boxes for the old free press. The rusting pumps. A bush of nettles. Rainbows in puddles –

These broken things you don't forget. These photos your brain takes.

Fell a long way our city, he thinks, looking down at these posh clothes and this bloody meat he's got for legs. A long, lengthy way. He looks up. Sees Noah coming back. Noah smirking.

But we're still scrabbling on the walls.

Noah gets in all lumpen, banging the door and blurring the coke in Brian's lap. Says, Shit – sorry mate. Only ham here as well; gutted.

Ham because pigs are the only things worth farming.

Brian, he looks at his life from a distance, on this forecourt, with these dreams and this tail. Polarity, animosity. Duality.

No handles to hold, no harness to lift.

He leans down –

Rails everything in the tray.

The pair of them, clipping from Manchester towards the Woodhead Pass at a flat sixty, Brian wired, half-cut, head out the window with a stomach turning over and over, too wired for nerves.

Noah is suited and booted, enjoying the corners, teaching Brian a different sort of line. Lines to learn; lines about his role in the war, where he served, who he served with. Noah's talking about gallows humour and one-liners for big grins, saying things like, Good things don't come in small packages, Brian. Letterbombs do.

They pass signs to Sheffield – green signs scrubbed and crossed through, overwritten with graffiti – A57 Crater one says. Never a good place to visit, everyone thinks. Rarer still to drive out this way, up and over the tops.

Manchester, that tall city in their mirrors, waits to turn on. Manchester, the shrinking city in their mirrors, quickly gone.

They hit the M67, windows flashing grey and flickering with shadows and skeletons from the foot bridges and bare bushes. Five miles of motorway to themselves. The hills loom closer, four PM on the nose, dusk falling by increments.

Rain clouds roll in to slate the biggest roof.

They cover the last stretch of unlit motorway and pay

their dues; pull away from the tolls by Hindley's Hattersley and edge downhill to dodge so many potholes. The fear of blockade gangs. No lights or holo-boards down this way. No cars either; nobody heading anywhere, the only noise from a couple of patrol levs whining over.

Through villages, grim grey villages – Shipman's Mottram, Tintwistle, all empty you'd think but full with ills – and on again, down and up, before the road cuts into dark green proper. Before the smell of death comes through all the windows. Before the rain can start.

Grim up north, says Noah, the Nissan pushing fifty in old thirty zones. About fifty more than it should manage, the way he drives it.

All around, the Pennines, these endless moors, crowd the car with long shadows. Once, it was a beautiful drive, the A628 – and not only if the light was right. It's thoroughfare, yes, a long bridge between Manchester and Sheffield, but to have so much green so close to a city was once seen as lucky –

Now, it's all weeds and damaged road surfaces. A ragged scar on the face of nature. Cracked tarmac scattered with bits of dry-stone walls pushed over by unpruned trees. And every hundred yards, an old orange SOS phone stands rotting, while the ghosts of freight lorries and tailgaters, the traffic you'd see here till four or five years back, echo and echo as memories.

The road winds on and up, ponderous. There's a funny camber to the corners. The men look into valleys, down into empty reservoirs; into the lay-bys and up the slab-sides of limestone. Ahead at the clouds, above at the trees. The rain chases them. And they see the walls with orange nets pinned on, the walls where people didn't brake soon enough. They remember dark stories of rapes and shallow graves. Imagine the dread –

The big open space makes for powerful wind. These hills are bleak; cold and shattered by gales.

How far from here? says Brian, chewing his face, gurning at the blackening sky with eyes cranked wide.

Flouch roundabout and a bit beyond, Noah says. Old farm buildings up that way.

Time we due?

Five, but can't roll in till Garland gives me the nod.

You know who you're looking for?

Aye. Two in particular.

He knows I'm with you?

No. And won't.

How come?

Because it's all about format. Let him think he's got me climbing drains. Romantic that way.

They're just past Flouch roundabout, towards Langsett, towards the M1 – the motorway you don't drive without armour or escorts. Past Flouch roundabout, on more winding roads to nowhere, when a pair of Defenders pull out in front.

Noah swerves, the offside bumper already gone up the wall. The car stalls, a wash of tyres over gravel – the whole thing as fast as that.

Next: three men in balaclavas, balaclavas with surplus army jackets; three men in balaclavas with guns. And Brian holds his ears, the coke biting now. Fear chewing his stomach out.

Rifles pointed through glass. Rifles and eye-holes, eyes and mouths, men barking, Out! Out the fucking car!

Noah and Brian raise their hands – that universal reflex.

Out!

Noah shouting, Easy! Easy!

39

Two men at the doors, gun barrels in two frightened faces.

While shepherds watch, one man says.

Another: Out fucking car, pair of you.

Noah spills from the door, stumbles out on to the road, looking back at Brian. Brian's trapped inside with both hands over his head; sweating and puffing, very red.

Gentlemen, the man in front of the car says, his rifle high. Not right road for you pair, this. Right turn were few mile back, actually.

We're –

Hush now. What's up with him in there, the man asks, pointing. Daft, is he?

He needs his wheelchair, Noah says. You've misunderstood. He can't get out, he's a –

The man kicks Noah's car. The hanging bumper rattles. The echo rolls.

Speak up, lad. Matter with you.

He's – he's disabled.

Mong, aye?

Where you off? asks one of the men.

Meeting. A meeting. And I'm his carer.

Meeting where?

There's a farm –

Get mong out the car, says one of the men.

Noah raises his hands. Noah protests. But he needs his chair, he says.

One man points to another, back to Noah.

Where you driven from? he asks.

Manchester.

And this meeting?

Noah's eyes narrow.

You know what I'm on about. Thinking, Yorkshiremen don't carry rifles like that for sweet F-A.

Open boot, the man goes. And say owt more you'll be swallowing teeth.

The man pointing a rifle at Brian pauses. Pauses and thinks. Thinks and moves, still pointing. He walks round the back of the car and opens the boot. The third man looks on.

He tuts.

Nowt here, he says to his pals, lying to his pals in balaclavas with their guns. No chair.

He points his gun at Noah. Noah begins to panic. He can think fast, Noah, but not like this.

In the car, Brian pulls the blanket from his lap. Brian opens the passenger door. Brian keeps his hands high. He hears the guns creak, sees the rifle tremble.

Brian puts a hand on the door. Pulls himself round. These aches and pains. The coke.

Brian slips on the door sill, falls to the ground hard, making a scene. Brian sits there, stunned and shaking and waiting for the crack.

The men laugh. The men point. Laughing and pointing as Brian sweats and crawls.

Got a name, has mong? Fuck's he doing?

Noah tries to stand. Wants to help Brian. His old buddy, his old pal. Brian crawling round the car, dragging his smart clothes and sorry bones across the tarmac.

Leave him be, says Noah. He's a soldier. A vet.

Soldier? says the man nearest Brian. This shite on floor?

The man rolls Brian on his back with his boot. The man notices Brian's body, the special shape in the special trousers – the ones Brian has for smart occasions. The ones now covered in grit and muck.

Brian, he's silent, still gasping –

Lads, says the man in the balaclava. Cunt's only got one leg!

The men start to laugh again.

Landmines were it? Landmines? Get lad up.

The man grabs Brian under his armpits. Tries. Tries harder. Up, fatty, he says.

Brian puts weight on his feet. Onto his fused, flattened feet. Feels himself pulled up; feels his armpits burning.

Brian leans heavy against the car door.

Noah's kneeling up now, angry and helpless. Hopeless. The man nearest asks what for. He says, Why you kneeling, cocker?

Noah says, Just look in the bloody glovebox. Medals are there. Falklands and the rest.

The three men in balaclavas look at each other, all eyes and mouths.

Brian slumps, sliding down, the man having to push him back up every few seconds.

The glovebox, Noah says again. We have somewhere to be. Better plans than this. There's cash in my pocket if you're after cash. I'm not a man to tell lies. Let him go – bloke deserves better than this. Let him go and see us on our way.

To go where?

To our meeting –

A meeting you've driven from Manchester for.

If you're security, you'll be off work tomorrow, says Noah. I can make sure. You know what I'm on about.

Now watch them lips and don't tell fibs, lad. Told you once. Idle threats aren't for keeping.

No fibs, Noah says. He's important, this bloke. Stocks and shares. Knew what's good for you, you'd do something else with your afternoon. Mither some other poor bastards.

Brian slides to his backside, too heavy now.

Red or blue? the man by Noah says.

What?

Red, or blue? Simple enough.

Quiet. The longest quiet.

Red.

Or.

Blue.

Blue, Noah says. True blue.

True blue – knowing all colours out this way are better than red.

Without a dream in my heart, he says.

The man in the balaclava shows his teeth. Greatest loss were national game, he says. Donny Rovers myself. What were last match you went?

City Blackburn, Noah says, snatching at names. March . . . 2011.

The man sniffs. Looks at Noah a while longer. The man nods. He points at the car. Check glovebox, one of you.

One of the men leans inside. Across blankets and spilled powder. Opens the glovebox. Pulls out tobacco tins and papers. Pulls out a medal – a medal with the Queen's profile, the blue and yellow ribbon. He picks out another medal – a yellow, blue and red ribbon.

Good fakes, Noah's thinking. The right kind of fakes.

A pause. Wide eyes bright in those holes to see.

Give over, the man in the car says. Not lying, were you?

So help him into the car, Noah says, pointing at Brian. Scared the bugger silly haven't you.

The man nearest Noah nods again.

Noah stands up and brushes himself down. Looks at the man straight. The man all eyes and mouth. A flinch now and the game's up. Flinch now and you're swallowing teeth.

The man in the balaclava sniggers. Looks away –

Were only joshing, you know, he says. Got to look out for these pakis an't we?

Noah smiles his thinnest smile.

Now skedaddle. 'Fore I change mind.

No, Brian's not all right. Brian's learning how fast you can sober. Gets to thinking about this mud on his trousers, these scuffs on his shirt. Grateful this once for a blanket round his legs – the warmth and the smell of damp wool.

They've moved a hundred metres. Noah's out the front, kicking seven bells out of the bumper. Muttering and running up, trying to get the rest of it off.

Noah pulls the whole thing off. Throws it over a wall.

Headlight's bust and all, Noah says, getting back in his seat. And what's that look for? Going on bloody expenses isn't it. Garland doesn't want to lend us a tank, Garland gets bills to settle.

Brian snorts.

Any road. Never met a good Yorkshireman, Noah says. Isn't anything good comes out of that bloody county. But we're right, son. We're okay.

Well if that was the welcome, Brian says to Noah, eyes still sore, what's the front door going to be like?

Wangle something, won't we, Noah says. Would've been different if we had a swish motor I reckon. Just bad luck. Bad luck and bad men.

Noah stops the car there. The engine ticks, clicks, choking oil.

Noah takes off his seatbelt and pushes the chair back. He says to Brian, Let's have a look at you then.

A look at what?

Noah does the once-over, poking and prodding. Noah frowns. Noah pulls a tissue from his shirt pocket and spits on it. Leans over and wipes muck off Brian's face – wipes away the dust.

Brian winces and pushes his hand. He says, Hell you doing? Get us halfway to killed, halfway up these moors, and now you're spitting on my face?

Noah laughs.

Tough at the top, kid, he says. You're a good man you are. A right bloody 'nana most of the time, but a good man. But I have to look after you don't I? So we'll do what we came to do, and we'll go home richer. For better or for worse.

Brian looks ahead. Gazing to hazy lights not far off.

Just have to trust me, won't you.

Brian still has snot down his chin. A polo of coke left on his left nostril.

So come on. Let's not be a fanny, says Noah. You're a soldier out this way, remember.

Brian goes to say something. Brian stops.

Brian's seen Noah reaching into the door pocket.

He watches Noah turn back with a can of something –

Does nothing, says nothing, feels nothing.

While Noah sprays him with air freshener.

Smells good that, Noah says, laughing a bit. Smells better.

And Brian looks back, at his eyes and at his mouth, tasting the air while smelling it – a bad crack at vanilla.

At Noah's face and hands.

Brian narrows his eyes. He calls Noah the worst word he can.

5.

Noah and Brian pile through a rotting fence on to a dead field. Into grass two feet deep – the old car up to its A-pillars in brown straw.

Noah's laughing at Brian's face. Tells him the reason's three-fold, and not to fret. Says, Son, here's why we're on this field.

They drive straight, wobbling, cutting new ditches through mud. Ploughing the field. Tilling the land.

What a man sows –

For one, Noah says, we're going round another way. Coming in from a direction we didn't really.

What's the bloody point? says Brian. He smells like bad soap. What's the point when them bastards back there already clocked us?

Nowt saying they're in radio contact, Noah says. Nowt saying they've not called ahead. He smiles then.

Second reason is I've rigged a mic to your chair and need to tell you about it –

Brian sniffs hard. Feels it in his throat. The drip. The sour taste.

Rigged my chair? When?

Doesn't matter when, he says. Ninja aren't I. But the signal's connected to your tape bank at home, plus a box in our boot. Failsafe's in your tie – they'll be running jammers if they're touchy – and the rest. So: you're running a closed circuit too. Local receiver's taped under your seat. A smart way to take notes if nothing else.

Brian shakes his head. Brian in his chair on the moors at the deepest end.

Third reason? says Brian.

Noah slams on the anchors. Noah spins them a hundred degrees. The car digs in, rumbling. Noah near as stalls it. Noah laughs, drums the steering wheel. Undoes his seat belt and lights up a fag. Noah pulls out his tie. Noah points at Brian's jacket, still swinging on a hanger from the back window.

Time to be a real Flash-Harry, he says. See how our little mermaid scrubs up.

From here it's another kind of fortress. The farm, that is. A stone cottage and a barn on a big plot with watchtowers for corners and grubby weather for cover. They pass it from the right, on the field still, seeing the compound over the privets. On all sides there are trees and high ground. Another place for men to run from something, to hide from the world.

Closer, they're back on the road now, coming from the other direction with bits of fence in the radiator probably. There's an extra building to goggle and gawp at. A low building, modern and brightly lit. Some daft assault course poking over the fence that runs round the whole compound – zip lines and poles, monkey bars and more.

By night, without these spotlights, you probably couldn't tell the place apart from others this way. From the other abandoned buildings. The dead squats at every turn. But now, here, in the deep end and pulling near, it's clockwork. Alive on all fronts. And humming.

Gates wide open; saw them coming.

Camera lenses smiling, hello to you.

Inner gates open, welcome to all.

Across the gravel and dry mud. Over grass and down a path. Over a cattle grid and round the back. A man in hi-vis waving them to where they should park.

The car park, it's a field and a fleet. Loaded with a fleet of better cars on hard-standing, most black and blacker still with tinted windows. Executive and then some. Lexus. Mercedes. BMW. The cars you knew those years before; cars that spoke or even sang of money. The clichés all the same, but forever the cars that say plenty about the men who drive them.

Between the cars, there are vans. Small business vans that carry tools for small projects. Vans with family names up their sides. For carrying people up on these moors –

And it's hard to miss the purple Transit.

Makes our Sunny look a right shit-tip, Noah goes, pulling the old motor round the stacked out rows, all stretching longways down the yard. The engine really clatters in second gear.

They find a spot between an Audi and a Beamer; swing too fast into the gap.

Brian is burning up, starting to sweat –

Noah forgets about second gear. Stalls it for certain this time. He grins and racks the handbrake, stretches and sits back. He slaps his cheeks and checks his teeth. Flattens his hair; fixes his jaw.

There's a purple Transit down the row.

Hold up while I get your chair, he says to Brian. You all right? Want a quick fag?

But Brian's pale, drowning, wanting to be elsewhere.

Noah gets out. Noah walks round the back. Noah comes round, leaning into the car. Passes Brian a hip-flask.

48

Have a toot of this. And get that polo off your conk. No more bloody sniff tonight, right? Not having you forgetting your lines on my watch.

They're bastards, these doormen. Even from fifty yards you can tell. Twenty-something kids in too-big suits. But like all the lads on the doors here and back in town, back in the basin below these hills, they get these jobs by default now, don't need trusting even. Not with shoulders wider than crash barriers.

Their shirt collars are tight, rolling their necks into their faces. They spit a lot.

Noah wheels Brian to the steps before them, tyres spitting gravel themselves. Here, at the entrance of the new building, they stop.

Brian's in his new jacket and war badges, the blanket tight round his legs. Brian with his bald head, sweating and forgetting his lines. Shaking. Waiting. His chest still crushed by the jacket.

Evening, says the doorman on the left. Polite but dripping with that accent. Your Christian names please, gentlemen.

I'm Kevin, says Noah. Just like that. Just like planned.

Noah puts a hand on Brian's shoulder.

This is Michael.

The doormen look at each other, down at their tablets. They tap screens and look at photos. They murmur under their breath. They umm and ahh.

Brian doesn't stir, doesn't look up once.

'Fraid we don't have you down mate, the doorman on the right says. He has a finger to his nostril, his eyes on Brian's war medals.

Noah opens his jacket to the doormen. Noah winks and chuckles.

49

Noah says, I know. Noah, his jacket wide open –
But God has laid us upon your hearts.

They enter the new development between double-doors
– doors like church doors. They're taken aback. The new
development, it's bubbling over. A space ahead, a lobby
in the centre, an atrium where men in suits stand in tight
circles, toasting whatever, chiming glasses and laughing
their heads off at crap jokes. From the atrium, the building opens outwards and upwards – to stairways on the
left and right leading to mezzanine gangways above.
There are rooms and hidey-holes, thick oak doors running either side of long corridors. Every floor is glazed
with glassy marble.

It's a maze, strip-lit and deceiving. A house of wrong
turns. A labyrinth.

Brian takes it in. Brian, lost with the minotaur.

Thinking about the driver of that damn purple Transit.

Brian's wheelchair squeaks on the floor since the rubber won't stick. Noah pushes him gently, purposefully;
keeps him near while they're met with champagne and
stares. As they're met with people chatting on, people
choking on their drinks. Fabulous, fabulous, they hear
on all sides. Superb and tremendous. Men proud of their
proverbs.

Noah leans in close, whispers: It's a bloody sausage-
fest.

The wheels lose traction. The wheels gain traction.

Somebody clocks the medals. The chair skating along.
Somebody wants to play philanthropist. A veteran! Brian
hears.

Somebody comes over. He's round and roly-poly, big
red cheeks on him. An honour sir, he says to Brian. An
honour.

50

Brian's stomach churns. Brian nods.

Here privately or for pressing business? the man asks. His eyes are set close, only just far enough apart.

Bit of both, says Noah, taking point.

Brian nods again.

The man shakes Brian's clammy hand. Tells Brian his name.

Brian doesn't listen.

The man tries with more small-talk. Brian doesn't speak back – doesn't speak at all.

Secrets best kept, Brian reckons.

Well, keep up the good fight, son, the man eventually says. Very much hope you enjoy this evening.

The man gives up with a wink and leaves them be.

Noah pushes Brian ahead and into the crowd. They keep having to stop and start and smile their thanks.

Excuse me, please, Noah says. Excuse us, cheers.

And from all corners the eyes of others are on their own – eyes poking out from the conversations and the executive patter; the deal closers and thoughts on the war. Conversations that change to cruel whispers of a spazz and his minder; the wounded soldier by there – over there, yes him, that's the one – him and his keeper.

The lion and the lamb.

Beyond the staring crowd, between the legs, beyond the backs, Brian can see another pair of church doors now. The auditorium, or so at least the signs say. They move forward. Slowly. Inching between the gaps. The backs always in his face. Thin-stemmed glasses swinging around at eyeball height.

And through the gaps, Brian sees him.

Sees the man in the corner.

The man staring back.

Another man from the margins. A man with a beard, a

51

beard and a slim suit, staring. A man staring and following their passage through suits, dodging wine glasses and elbows. A man watching and waiting for something.

Brian feels studied. Brian feels hot.

The man in the gaps doesn't blink. His face flickers as Noah weaves Brian through this forest of men. Gone and there. Vanished and waiting as Brian's view cuts fast between arms, over sleeves, the Vs cut by legs.

Brian looks away. Brian pretends he hasn't noticed. Looks sidelong. Looks back.

The gaze doesn't falter.

Ten metres now. Less.

Sweating. Blinking. Adrenaline. Something wrong. Noah isn't noticing and Brian can't make a scene.

Outside, the night tips fully into black.

Into the auditorium. It's a narrow room but tremendously long. Bigger here than it looks outside and no mistake – all Victorian details and garish curtains. A kind of theatreland. A theatreland beyond the noise and the lights.

Hidden back here with the red-backed chairs and the sticky floors, it's quieter. The odd bod sitting in a chair here and there.

It's not completely quiet though. There's some god-awful music on the PA. Big jugs of water down the front. The stage is small – barely a few metres wide – and the lectern is stained wood, handsome.

An usher sees Brian and Noah. He's dressed up like a twat. He jogs along the aisle and tells them to head down the central ramp. He makes some uncomfortable joke about disabled parking at the front. He laughs and skips away. Noah chuckles. Noah points two fingers at the usher. Cocks with his thumb.

Come the revolution, brother, he says to Brian, and wheels Brian down the incline, between the rows.

Brian tips his head back, looking up at the smooth, smooth ceiling. His heart's going like the clappers. He says, Something's wrong, Noah. Everything's wrong.

Eh? Give over, goes Noah. What's this now?

I saw something. Somebody. I don't know; I feel –

Like you've had a G of dust's how you feel, Noah says. Talk a long talk, don't you our kid. Just sit still and wait this out. Tape'll be running now – can't be filling it up with this clap-trap.

Noah parks Brian just three feet from the stage edge.

There, he goes. These are the perks. Knew this'd be a good idea.

But Brian's thinking too hard to enjoy perks; thinking too fast and too loose. Who was he, why is he here what does he want with me –

Noah comes round his front and straightens the badges at Brian's breast. Asks if they're right yet, him and him. If they're ready to kiss and make up.

Brian doesn't nod. Brian doesn't shake his head. Noah takes it as encouragement.

The pair of them sit at the foot of the stage. Brian imagines so many eyes upon his back. Eyes that drill and mine and bore above the whispers, under the hot stage lights.

Sitting under the foot of a new world taking aim.

Brian, a thorn among nails.

6.

Bob on six, the room grows quiet. Filled, still filling; hushed and hushing. And he walks on then, their man. Flash suit, no tie. Sharp shiny shoes, no stubble. A good six feet longways, taller by the angle.

Noah nudges Brian. Noah has a notepad and a pencil. Noah angles the notepad so Brian can see. He's written a single word. A short, nasty summary.

Brian fidgets, still too warm.

Their host taps his microphone, feeding back a little. He gestures upstairs, taps again. Thumbs up. A better volume. He looks into the crowd. He has hand on his brow, smiling at all he sees – this room already feeling like his kingdom and his glory.

They clap and whistle.

Gentlemen, their host says. Or one hopes at least most of you are. A warm welcome to my home. To this evening.

Clapping.

It is my privilege – it's always a privilege – to collect you and your colleagues in this room. To your left, and to your right, you see the ambitious. The ruthless. The arrogant, be as that may. But not the wrong. Never the wrong.

Clapping.

It is my privilege to provide an alternative, up in these hills, their host says.

Of course, we have the watchtowers outside, our watchtowers and our armed friends from all over the North. And there is sharpline, yes. Strong barriers against the great unwashed beyond our view.

But here, in these hills, I have created a clearing; a clearing in which the tendrils of their councils will cast no shadow. And I'm honoured because we – we, in this room – represent a new private sector, my friends.

Their host puts his hands together. Flexes his fingers against fingers. Listens to the clapping.

We are the entrepreneurs, now. Entrepreneurs in a time where contracts are secured only by traitors and the hive-mind that runs our city. Entrepreneurs in a stagnant state – a state in stasis. A state that has wilfully starved our companies' development and stolen some of our finest to shore up their own.

Their host pauses. He frowns. He raises his voice.

We are here because the city does not want us. Because the council has found its own way – through martial law and through terror. Through lying and through spying. Taking our intellect and with it our property.

But my friends, no longer. My friends, there are people who *do* want us. Those who'll give us the means to create a better way. Because now, we have donors and benefactors from all over this globe – men from here and abroad who recognise that to save our country, we need strength. Technological strength. Moral strength.

It will not be a coup we create. It will be a true and righteous progression. Progression from an economy we none of us benefit from. From a society that stumbled during the riots. Stumbled in the decades before them. And is still down and out.

Their host paces. Paces along and around his stage, the audience in his hands. Him in their hearts.

55

Their host continues. He says, The things we showcase here, we will sell. We will outsell our competition – perhaps even each other. And in selling, we will arm a financial struggle against our state. This state that has allowed the enemy in, and the enemy to flourish.

This state built on corruption and filthy backhanders. A state built on intervention and wars we've no need to fight. A state that has burnt international bridges, turned off our internet. A state that has left our infrastructure to entropy, our satellites to fall.

A state not built on honour, nor Britishness.

Clapping –

Roaring, in fact –

Their host smiles to his crowd.

Their host traces a circle round the auditorium with a single fingertip.

You may have noticed the cameras around this room. These cameras are sending images of this stage to those friends of ours elsewhere. Sending a message by the satellite we've hijacked to our friends upstairs. That is why I ask that you do not see any of the men that follow me up here as a keynote speaker. Don't listen to the words of any one man and mistake them as part of some keynote address.

This is your forum. Our forum. This is where we show the country how we can take back the industries we helped to build.

This venue is where you, representing the companies our state will no longer buy from, have your chance. This venue is one of many in this country where similar words are resonant.

Do they know we're here? Undoubtedly. I would wager we have their agents amongst us this evening. That's fine by me. They say we are a democracy, so let them listen. Trust me when I say they will not act for fear of looking weak. They are weak, and that is why they will not act.

I know there's a feeling among you that time is against us. That without our old communications and without free motorways, we are short on resources, too. Tonight, however, I will introduce a series of men who say differently. Men who will say that both time and resources are yours; yours alone. We can be patient in this decaying city, this dying country. Patient because your ideas will brighten it all.

Their host stops. Their host looks down at Brian on the front row. Brian with his shaved head, in his chair. His chair at the centre of this world.

Brian sweats. Wants to throw up. Brian shrinks into his seat. Into himself. Wants to pull his blanket over his head. Wants nobody behind to see.

His lies. Their lies. A road too far.

Their host points at Brian from the stage –

Noah grins. Noah smiles. Noah laughs. Noah getting what he wants and more.

Look at this man. We're doing all of this for the men our state has betrayed. Like this brave gentleman here. Because God himself smiles on our war.

The room claps violently for Brian.

Their host looks on, eyes glassy. Their host is smiling.

Please enjoy your evening.

From the PA comes a circus of bluster. On the stage, a cycle of tall men with agendas written on the back of their hands.

Never again, Brian's whispering to Noah. Seething. Too far by half this, he's saying.

Noah is making notes. Noah's listening to the men on rotation on a platform three feet above.

Shush up you mopey bastard, he says. You're doing just fine. Kidded him, didn't you.

Only Brian wants the bar. Beers and chasers. Cigarettes. Joints. The end of bloody days.

And the men, they keep coming. Coming out to the handsome wood podium, photocards on ribbon round their necks, to talk about problems and solutions. Strategies, profit margins, expansion. Engineering by Great British engineers. Words that don't mean much, but words that still raise applause.

They've built robots for agriculture. Stainless robots for rich, free farmers. They've built new machines to manufacture better field guns. Bomb disposal units. Bombs altogether. Panic rooms. Micro IR cameras for God-knows-what and God-knows-where.

These entrepreneurs. These captains of industry.

Brian watches them all while Noah sits next to him, scribbling in his notepad.

Brian falling on some kind of savage comedown. On some kind of comedown already – the coke bad, the headache worse. The walls bending and buckling and closing.

Brian, who's yet to hear how they'll help him walk.

War has always been good for state business, the men say on stage. War drives medicine, civil engineering, weapon technology. War drives exploration.

War is a business, other men say. And it's time we shared the spoils again.

Why would you attack the Beetham? other men ask. What's the philosophy of civic attacks, and where's the causality? They're exploring the point; the purpose.

Beetham Tower was not an economic target, other men say. Bringing it down didn't disrupt national interests. Manchester Piccadilly would have been a better target.

And the acolytes simply go on clapping. Noah and Brian both thinking of the advert Noah put at the top of that tower.

Luddites bombed our museum of science and industry, other men say. They bombed what the Beetham tower could not touch as it fell. They bombed heritage to free themselves. They bombed it because they're not proud of the cotton mills. Not proud of the chimneys, of Lowry or the waterwheels. The canals and the pigeons –

We have technologies to stop these atrocities, the men on stage say. And they're getting better all the time.

Noah nudges Brian. Noah yawns. Noah passes Brian his notepad.

Need a slash, the page says. Don't be swanning off.

Brian's neck won't stop itching from all the eyes.

And Noah does one. Brian hears him jog up the central aisle. Out through the double-doors already.

On the stage, a man says, Terrorism is changing. Civil war is coming.

Brian doesn't know about that –

Brian takes the pad from Noah's empty seat. Reads that page. Reads other pages. Notes and notes, bulleted lists with bits underlined twice. Sort of methodical, despite the messy writing. Like Noah's bunker. Like Noah's plans.

The words from the stage blur. The men on stage turn featureless. The words fade out and away. Brian reads on, the notes screaming in figures and projections. And Brian wonders what they're for. Why they're needed when this tape's turning slowly under his seat.

Brian takes the biro. Brian writes –

Boredom bores boring bores bored.

He looks up once, gathering thoughts, a man on the stage babbling on, the pen moving to his mouth –

59

Then:

A touch. Burning synapses.

Somebody tapping Brian's shoulder.

Brian jumps. Wonders just what the hell's going on.

A piece of folded paper comes over his collar. He hears the whispers, quiet whispers in these shadows at the foot of the stage.

A quiet voice. Slightly effeminate.

Don't turn round –

I said, *don't.* Don't turn around, Brian. Don't look at me. Don't act like I'm talking to you –

What?

Somebody wants to see you.

What? says Brian. What?

Read the note.

Brian and this sick feeling. That same sick feeling.

Interval, the note says. Thick ink, a marker pen or something. Go for your piss and your cigarette and we'll find you.

Brian folds the paper back up. Stuffs his pocket with it. Says, What's going on?

See you in a bit, says the voice. Just wait for the bell.

On the stage, the voices singing those old executive songs. Solutions for problems the world doesn't even have.

The bell doesn't come. Brian's already left the conference. He struggled up the auditorium central aisle while so many eyes turned, saw him, and looked away. The atrium, lobby, foyer, however you want to spin it, it's cooler than back in there. There's a breeze from twin air-con units – the strong and silent types.

Brian wheels through, his chair squeaking a bit. Nobody really about. Pair of bouncers by the entrance doors, running their mouths. They quieten on seeing him, like most do. They ask where he's off to.

Brian holds up his baccy tin. Ears still roaring. Wishing he were home, thinking of straws and white lines on glass. Wondering where Noah got to, actually.

The bouncers smile and hold the doors for him. These gentlemen and this gentleman. Duty-bound by sympathy – some kind of pity for the sort of man who can't open doors for himself. Or at least bound by Noah's bribe.

His cig break, in truth a cig with a bit of weed, feels like a reward for his efforts. There's a funny sort of near-silence outside, the quiet with the bright stars. The floodlights are off, see, so he can look to bright constellations you won't see back home. To stars you miss in the city. And all about him, in the car park, are the vans and cars, the vans with family names up their flanks. Names with the dates local businesses were born. The bastards who own them back inside; all these bastards in one room. Over to the west, he can see the glow of Beetham Memorial.

And all this out here, with this cig with a little bit of weed in it, as wind runs over distant cars, distant wheels ploughing gravel. Wondering what the hell anybody would want with him, anyway.

Fag on. Fag off. Burning red to grey to dead. An about-turn. Funny to watch, if anybody could.

Brian says, Thank you, as the gatekeepers with their fat necks hold the doors again.

Of all the pissers in all the world, Brian just had to roll into this one. Right into the man from the lobby. The staring man from the atrium who's drying his hands, adjusting his tie.

61

Another thing with Brian, in his wheelchair, is that he's hard to miss. Hard to miss and harder to ignore. So the man doesn't ignore him. And Brian thinks, All these things colliding, these people in this place. The coincidences – the way you bump into everybody you least want to. Like he's the pivot of the whole thing.

Coincidences. These walls tighten and buckle and close. Brian's mouth has turned all cotton-woolly.

The man doesn't speak, as it goes. The man just walks around Brian without even looking at him – makes him think he's lost the plot besides. Which probably he has, in fairness. A long while back.

But the man has second thoughts. The man turns back, like he's forgotten his keys or something.

He says to Brian, Wish me luck, won't you?

And he's gone again.

And Brian can't piss at a urinal, can he. Has to use a cubicle. Picks the third one down. Farthest away. Wondering just what the hell's going on. Dizzy thinking where Noah is. Wondering what anybody wants with Our Brian, here, pretending to be a goddamn soldier who fought in these wars he knows absolutely sod-all about.

Brian has to park his chair at the door, prop the door with it. The door is very loud as it slams the wall. Brian has to stand up and sort of wedge himself diagonally between the plywood – shoulders on one side, his meat for legs on the other. His jacket flaps open and his medals jingle.

Brian struggles with his flies. Eventually, he pulls himself free. Diagonal in the cubicle and fiddling an awful lot with his penis.

And Brian can't reach down to lift the seat, can he. So he just goes all over it.

Brian's piss is dark brown. That old liver packing up,

he shouldn't wonder, though more likely that he's dehydrated. And the poor lighting come to that. But he never drinks enough water, does he. He knows because Diane tells him when she ruins his life every Thursday.

Our Brian, who's lodged in the cubicle all diagonal, pissing treacle, when others come in and see his empty chair. Others who think something terrible's gone off in the bogs.

Brian the centre of attention, again. This bloody useless bastard slouched on a plywood divider.

Face round the corner goes, Hello? You all right mate?

Brian's hot and faint. Still pissing. Shaking with the weight of himself, his meat wanting to give way at the ankle joint.

Fuck off! Brian says. Fuck off!

Mate –

Brian wriggles and frets and falls backwards into the chair, which flashes back into the sink and leaves Brian prone on the wet tiles, his nob hanging out, his head propped on the chair's edge.

Centre of bloody attention. And these blokes pick him up and put him away in his chair. Fold him in half and say, We simply came to collect you, sir. Meeting, we believe. Haven't you?

Like some good soldier never left behind.

Their host has a converted shipping container and that's where Brian goes. That's where he's taken by the men from the toilet. Through more double-doors and down corridors, round the outer curve of the auditorium and out the back.

He has sweaty hands and a leaden belly. Clanging up a ramp with a lot of unsettled feelings and a single thought:

Shit.

Their host has a cigar on; his feet on the table. Pretending like he's a mobster, basically, in his pinstripes and his tan brogues. Reclining half-arsed in his Chesterfield. Worn-out fictions colouring new life on the moors. A relic of the 80s; of time-share and yellow Porsches. Coke and sinking pinks, every night; every bloody night.

Their host is a pretend mobster in a shipping container with flaking paint and creeping rust. Over the moors, the wrong side of Sheffield. A bad world going worse.

Their host is wreathed in smoke, sitting here among his papers and his pens. Beneath the low ceiling and a simple lamp shade. He lowers his glasses, flashes his peepers. Good to actually meet you, he says, watching Brian by the ramp. Brian who is sweaty and fat and yellow-fingered.

He coughs. My name is Ian.

I know, Brian says. Brian bluffing. He didn't know.

I'm Michael, Brian says. Pleasure.

I know, says Ian. Not bluffing. Eyeing what Brian has for legs.

So come in, come in, Ian says. Glad I caught you actually. Stuck out a little down front, didn't you; thought I'd introduce myself.

Brian nods. Brian seems all right with that. Even if he's still a bit wet from the toilet floor. A bit red and headachey.

Tea? I find all good things start with a decent brew.

I'm all right, Brian says. He can't help feeling that he's acting shifty.

How's about a Chai tea then?

I don't think so, ta.

It's really just spicy Horlicks, Ian says. You remember Horlicks, don't you? He says Horlicks without the H.

Brian nods.

Course. Weren't born yesterday.

Ian takes his feet from the table. Half as if to show off his good manners, half to prove something.

No, he says. None of us were.

Ian has boiling water on tap. A small unit at the far corner of his desk. Brian watches Ian pour himself a stout brew. Yorkshire Gold on the teabag. Stockpiled or something, because you can't buy that stuff now.

Ian studies Brian's fake war medals.

I remember the army, says Ian. All them bare walls, the pool room brawls.

Well, me too, says Brian.

Taught me how to spot liars, did the army. Spot liars and shoot wogs any road.

Brian nods. Tries hard not to wince.

Still. Got lucky, you getting out with that.

Should've seen the other guy, Brian says, the lies thick in his mouth.

RPG?

Something like that.

Well, all I can say is resentment's a good fuel.

You get your moments, Brian says.

Are you a nationalist, Michael?

Brian pulls a face, awkward –

Ian puts his hand up. Smiles.

It's all right, he says. But come with me a moment, will you? Got something to show you.

Ian rolls Brian along his neat lawns. There's a gravel path, but he cuts it out, nodding to the odd group of men they pass. The grass is anyhow short enough for a comfortable ride.

Like my house, Michael?

Very impressive, says Brian.

Makes a superb fairway, you have to say.

I can't – don't play golf.

Never supposed you did. But it's home, aye.

Soon they reach an old bandstand, open and ramped at one edge of the hexagon. Ian pushes Brian up and on to the decking – whitewashed and remarkably clean. In the centre of the bandstand, there's a pond, under-lit with gentle blue bulbs and looking tidy also. It looks deep. A small stone cherub, penis in hand, circulates silver water. A filter buzzes in the corner.

They sit at the edge, Brian leaning forward, Ian taking a bench.

Oranges, whites, silvers, foot-long and flowing, crowd together and break the water's surface. The fish with gawping mouths and slow eyes.

Keep forever, these lot will, says Ian.

They're – they're very nice, says Brian.

Could watch them all day, Ian says. Man needs his pursuits, doesn't he? If it in't women any road. Had these boys ten year already. Camera up there to watch on cooler days, shall we say. Plus roof keeps birds out, doesn't it.

Brian nods.

Planned a lot out here, says Ian. See these as my panel. Don't answer back, do they? Simple living for simple beings. And we all know manners maketh man.

Brian nods again; smiles thinly as Ian chuckles at himself. He spots a thick black koi, possibly the only in there.

Shame we don't have it easy like these.

Mm, says Brian.

Course, in winter, deep winter, you wonder if they'll survive under ice. Haven't let me down yet though. But what's interesting, right, is their temperature depends on temperature outside. Clever, that. Right bloody cunning. Means they get through cold months by doing bare minimum.

Right, says Brian.

Our country works same way.

I don't really –

Michael, Michael, listen. In these colder months, years, we're just getting by. But imagine what we could do if we all rubbed up against each other. Got all heated up for a bit of graft.

Ian puts out his hands, draws an imaginary line from one edge of his land to the other.

Hard work. That's what it's all about.

Back in the container, the electric heater's on.

Ian waves his men out and sits back in the Chesterfield, opening a top drawer. He pulls out an envelope – a dirty, dog-eared envelope. He slits its neck and opens it wide. Shakes out the contents: photos in black and white.

Ian says, Roll yourself a bit closer, will you Michael?

Soon Ian has spread the photos right across his desk. He takes a moment to neaten the edges so they're straight and parallel.

Have a scan of these, he says.

Brian cops a look. Brian recognises the scenes. Everybody would, and everyone does. The same scenes they burnt into your brain for year on year after the fact.

Deansgate after the fall. Before the column of light. The way they wanted this to be iconic. A bigger event than the IRA managed in '96. The ironies and the pratfalls. The government who caused it. A government who decried it.

This is the day I became nationalist, says Ian. The day forty-seven bastard floors fell onto GMEX were same day

I woke up. All of us here like sleeping giants back when.

Brian nods. Brian gets that. Knows it was the start of something in more ways than many.

More than Oldham, 2001. Bradford, 2001. Moss Side, 1981.

More than The National Front. The English Defence League. The Red National Front. The lads on Strangeways roof. Rangers on tour, 2009.

Here's a storyboard for the riots. The war in pictures. The end of waiting; the start of acting. The prologue.

Are you a nationalist, Michael? Ian repeats. Is that why you snuck into my conference? To help our cause?

Brian shakes his head, then nods. Says, I don't know. Says, I don't get what you're after –

Just a question, isn't it?

Mam said you love this country in spite of this country.

The walls buckling, tightening, choking.

What's that? You're mumbling.

I said, Mam said you love this country in spite of this country.

Well then, goes Ian. She were wise, your mam. Might be on to something. But me, I were there, on Deansgate. There to see. Were standing there with our kid, just seven he were. Me, well, like me now but younger. Outside where Harrod's used to be. Remember everyone round me, don't I. Coppers over the road. Bloke rolling a fag. And a bunch of Muzzers – pram with their dad. Twin buggy, two more for the cause or what?

Lights go off first, black-out right down road. Like a corridor. Whole street shakes. No screams either, not like you'd think. And it went down fast – sand castles in the sea I thought, have thought since. Like sand. And then the dust. Ha! Rolls like a bastard when it's that hot, son.

You felt shockwave, sure, but heat on your face. Deansgate were a tunnel, and all this dust flies at us. For us. Screams now and people running, people running with arms off, grey faces with dripping features. The copper's fucking screaming that we do one, running himself. The kid with rolling baccy's on his arse, head in hands.

But thing was, when that building came down, the noisiest thing you ever heard, I saw something. Everything's gone to shit, right? And yet I saw that paki with kids shout something. God is great, he said. And he smiled – he's smiling. So when the dust comes over us, coughing, grey, coughing bits of people you realise later, I go for him. Feel for his face and take my chances. Twat him between eyes. Bop him on the sweet spot. He goes down and I'm stamping on his head like grapes in barrels.

Jesus, says Brian. That's –

Seen buildings levelled, have you? Well this was a levelling. Only shame is footage we got came off security grid.

Brian doesn't know what to think.

Ian laughs. Points at Brian's meat.

I'm surprised you're surprised, he says. Weren't Tinkerbell who did that to you, were it?

Brian shrugs.

Plus we've always been a racist lot, our country. Dirty words, dirty thoughts. Fearing the unknown, whatever they say. You sit next to a mud on the train back in the days before, and you're half thinking he's going blow you out the fucking window. Difference now is, we've got balls to say it. Aren't dirty thoughts when they're out for all to see. Not after what they did. What they do. Riots, whatever else. Nothing unknown about that shower of bastards.

Media that, though –

Don't give me that, Michael. I'm just asking where your head falls at night. How you dream. Fighting your long wars out in that place that took your leg, or back here, with the people who care about your country and where it's gone. Where it's going.

I –

Ian stands up. Slams his hands on the table and leans, leers. You bloody nothing, he shouts. I'll ask you one more bastard time. Are you, Michael, a nationalist? Is that why you're taping my conference? Bribing my door staff with that skinny runt you brought up here with you? Or are you having me on?

The voice falters. Brian's. He hears himself cracking up.

I love this country in spite of this country, he tells Ian –

Ian smiles. Teeth out. Teeth white. Ian sits down.

Ian says, Good job an' all. Because it is men like us who form that bulge out to sea. Because soon that sea will deliver her progeny, and the enemy will find out whether all these rumours about the Anglo-Saxons are true. Men like us – like them back in that room – are the foot-soldiers. Me and you, we are the wave, rushing inland to save all. Because, Michael, they're winning the war in the maternity wards, and we'll make sure we win on streets. Crusaders, all of us. Sons of Albion – all of us. And we'll drive out these craven forces. We'll build a good future for our lads and lasses. Crosses and not crescents.

Crosses not crescents, Brian breathes, his ears roaring. Thinking of the Cat Flap and the girls who lie there. Their pigtails and their fingernails. Of Diane and her care. Of Tariq in his taxi.

Of the riots over whatever the riots were over.

Man like you'll help spread the message, says Ian.

70

Show our country what real men think of this government and the trouble it's lumped us with. 'Cause everybody likes to be part of something, don't they? People we
know, well they'll fix you up. The man the government
stole a leg from. The man our resistance gave a leg back
to.

Brian looking down. Thinking. Torn between vomit-
ing hard and the guilty attraction of it.

Thinking, Where's Noah bloody got to?

Ian flames his cigar. Pulls half a centimetre in and
blows a stormcloud back out.

Now then. Business. Who's that rat you're with?

Brian fidgets and forgets his lines. Can't remember the
name Noah gave himself.

He's a friend, Brian says. Looks out for me.

Seems interested in our business, says notepad of his.
Not one of these silly hacks – not an activist, is he?

Just a good pal. Like I said.

And your recorder? Thing taped under your chair?

Saves me carrying it.

Ian laughs. Ian's face bloody splits.

Well look at us, says Ian. A cripple with his opportunity, a kingmaker before him. But you know, lies aren't
becoming, Michael – that's what *our* mam said. And my
quarrel's simple, really. Few lads saw you come in. Not
talking them no-neck meatheads on door either. And
these lads reckon he's got a shop in your city. Pills and
rest. Reckon he used to go ambient. Might still be freelance. Doesn't care who he works for, does he? Council
lads, council coppers. Lads in my industry. Decent CV
by all accounts though.

Brian's wheelchair squeaks. Soft fibres crushed from
left to right.

I don't know anything about that, says Brian.

71

Course you don't, son. But throw a cushion long enough, Michael, and the zip'll hit someone in eye.

I mean, I don't get what you're saying.

Not saying a lot. Just wary of that cunt aren't I? Enough that you both snuck your ways in here. Still. He'll be wondering where you've got to.

Brian nods.

Expect he will. Anyone left to see out there?

Ian looks at his watch. Taps it.

Aye, a few, he says. Some enterprising bastard turning car plant machinery into walker tech. Ian plays his poker face. The hook, the line, the sinker.

Really? says Brian, the reflex getting the better of him. So much so that for that split second, he thinks, Fuck Noah and Garland anyway.

Ian reaches over the desk with a card.

Take this with you. Want to talk to me again, call this number. It's a redirect, so don't be put off if it throws your call around a bit. Suffice to say I've had files wiped off that thing under your arse.

Brian pockets the number. Rocks in his chair and turns clockwise. Tick tock. Time running slow, running thick.

Oh, and wheels?

Brian doesn't turn back. He's on the way from the room by this ramp. It's dark out, now. Dark and grisly – the air gone wet.

What would you have done, if you saw that sand-coon smiling at the end of our city's tower?

Brian stops. Thinks. Watches the dust roll across the floor.

Why?

Just want to know. That people-dust in your eyes. The smells. Your seven-year-old brother cut up and bleeding in your hands.

72

Brian says, I would've done nothing. I wouldn't have been able to reach.

Back in the house that Ian built. Into this home where you're easily lost.

Into a house of eyes – a room of seats and enduring stares. Down that central aisle. The hush loud while the man on stage rants and raves about this and that.

Brian sees Noah back in his place. He stops short of his feet and whispers, Miss me?

Noah ignores him. Brian stops still.

Ships in the night, Brian says.

Piss off, Noah goes. You've gone and diddled us. Told you to stay bloody put, didn't I?

There's sweat on brows, on stage and off. Brian's meat is burning with itches and stress. He should've remembered nylon mix never sits well over split skin.

But they're on to us. Have been since we got here –

I know.

They know about your council chums. Jobs you done. That Garland's a lobbyist. And they've wiped our tape –

I know. I know. Just shut up. Tell me what happened later.

We should get off.

No. Camera at one o' clock. Don't look at it you daft bastard. It's aimed at the pair of us –

Clapping explodes behind them. It rolls side to side, back to front.

This last few and we're out, says Noah, raising his voice now.

A fat man lolls off stage to cheers and more.

Just don't leave my sight.

Brian eyeballs his lap, his tie like a fat arrow to all that's wrong.

The clapping picks up again as there's some introduction, some chatter.

And on the stage, the staring man – the man from the toilet – walks out.

Brian stares and stares and stares.

Turns to Noah with, My days, that's him.

Hello, says the man above. Thanks. Thanks –

It's a pleasure, the man says, holding up his hands. Cheers. But you'll stop clapping when I say I need some help. Not got long, so I won't beat around the bush. Oh, and I'm Colin. It's really good of you to listen so late in the evening – and after so many great ideas, too.

Brain stares and thinks and panics.

He's smaller up there on the stage, this Colin, and doesn't so speak loudly either. When he does it's to say something too fast. Obviously not a natural like these others. Doesn't seem interested, even. The tie too straight. The shoes too shiny. Like only earnestness got him this far. Like only a louder mic could take him further.

Probably many of you held public contracts before the renationalisation programme, Colin says. And we all know it stung. I mean . . . I mean you've had these grants – the 2016 grant for one – but tokenism hasn't helped. Doesn't build stuff, right? Your satellites are breaking up, phones networks gone, cables degrading, roads falling to bits. Things aren't great. Which . . . which I guess is why you're all here.

Get on with it, someone shouts.

Well, I've come a long way, Colin says. Haven't done this much, either. But I've come a long way to say this, which I also haven't really done before. And it's going badly, right? Yeah, properly badly so far.

I need help. Materials and investors. Same kind of

74

things you all want. But I need it for something you haven't seen or heard of.

I'm from a long way off. Asking for investment in something I've seen myself – that only a lot of brains together could build.

So what I'm asking is, what if we build links with other worlds? I don't mean scattering out to space, or rockets, or anything else. I mean closer to home. I mean alongside our own – parallel to our own? Cooperation and trade, a network of resource pathways. Because it's my belief we'd become stronger widthways. It can't just be about running the long length of time.

People are looking between themselves, baffled, and asking who the hell this guy is. No warm up or setup. No pitch. And now this nonsense.

People start laughing.

And somehow Colin grows bolder. You'd prefer me to talk about space, would you? Not the spaces between? Chat on to you in the numbers you know, the maths you live by. But I'm here to say it's more than that.

Colin holds up a box and opens it. A little steel box it looks like. He points inside – it's empty.

Me, I found a fuel, a gate, a chance. Found a chance for all of you.

And the laughter turns to booing and jeering. To a pantomime –

Colin the man who's brought an idea nobody can believe in.

Brian staring up at Colin, this man, the staring man, who asked Brian for luck in a toilet and needed it.

But somebody's interested. Somebody someplace. Because all of the cameras, all of them studding the auditorium walls, are turned and trained on the skinny young man – the man with a beard and his box – on the stage.

7.

The cameras. The shot. The screams.
  The cameras. The blood. The panic.
  The cameras. The wound. The scramble.
  The cameras. The hands. The chaos.
  The cameras.
  The auditorium.
  The end.
  Brian was close enough to see. The bullet went in and
the bullet back came out. So fast, too – the jacket shoul-
der bursting, black curtains twitching, this gangly man
going spastic on the floor. And now, Noah has pulled
Brian's head down and close; pushed his face towards
his knees.
  Colin is fully splayed, down and out on his stage
above.
  And everybody is running under harsh house lights –
harsh and white, the crowd in fragments.
  Brian babbles. Brian wants to shit. Brian shouts.
  Noah's behind now, his rough hands on the foam handles. Up the ramp with Brian on point, the pair of them
dodging men as they hurdle chairs towards the doors,
some tripping, some smashing their mouths on the next
chair along.
  More shots, that smell of animal fear. Noah shoves his
head down by Brian's shoulder, sprinting, all his weight
against the chair and the angle of the slope. You can hear

his breath punctured when his feet catch their grip.

Noah pushes Brian through bodies in flight. All the while, Brian screaming, Out the way, out the bloody way.

Into the lobby, and more shots ahead. Plaster swirls in a fine powder, grey and loose. It's the doormen this time, pistols over their heads, as a hundred men tear-arse towards doors only built for the width of two. That noise and fear; confusion and fights; the selfish gene, the ruthless escapes –

Stop here and you'll catch men trampling to avoid the crush, their hands on others' scalps. You'll see how turned ankles can make piles of men.

Into the night, dozens and dozens of feet over the gravel. The bastards all sprint on to the car park, kicking up loose stones which skip into bodywork.

Only Brian and Noah are caught short by the doors on account of Brian's chair. Elbows rain from all places – men on men over men. Noah has his arm creased around Brian's head, some kind of fleshy visor. And then people are going over the wheels, a wonder there aren't fingers caught in the spokes. Stuck fast. Stuck sure.

There's a squash as the force behind begins to build. The pressure swells as more bodies funnel up at the back. Suddenly Brian comes free, fast, while Noah stumbles – the pair of them exploding into cold northern air like corks from the fizziest bottle.

Drive. Just drive, shouts one of them to the other. Both of them caught hard between the buzz and the bite. The driver. The passenger. The chair slung in the back. The murder they saw, a shooting they survived.

Noah's shaking. Brian, too. Drive. Just bloody drive. First gear, not reverse – fuck! Reverse, out, front wheels spinning and kicking up chips.

Noah is shaking. Noah's jaw flaps loose and fast. This motor-mouth giddy and halfway to screaming. The adrenaline's really going. Plus don't forget, only a single headlight's working –

Noah pulls away. Out. Faster cars pulling round them. What did they do here?

Light me a bloody fag, says Noah, manic. Light us a pair of bloody fags will you –

And Brian lights up, passes the cigarettes. The car on the road – out among the black cars and white vans, headlights, tail lights. Round Flouch roundabout and back on Woodhead. Past that bombed out pub and round the cracks.

Noah winds his window, nudging forty, scarcely braking. Harsh drags and strong smoke.

Giddy up, you bastard, he shouts.

Shouts and starts to laugh.

Another mile and calmer by then, the rain coming down harder now. It's raining so hard, in fact, they can hardly see – just the road out front and the wet black, squinting out. The wipers grind over windscreen glass, the motor ringing loud – a grim metronome. Bang to the left and to the right. Bang to the left and to the right.

That was fucking insane, says Noah, still grinning.

What do we do?

Back to Manchester, says Noah. Home and safe.

He spoke to me, didn't he?

Who?

The staring bloke – Colin.

Lad who got shot?

Aye.

Eyes forward. Jaw set. Back to their city as fast as you like. Back home with memories to keep. Silent for the bleak winds and bitter night. Thinking of poor Colin, arm blown out. Of what to say about it. Baths and blood and hair and meat –

Coincidence, you think?

Bloody hope so, says Brian.

Poor bastard.

And Ian had his say-so, did he? His tuppence?

All sorts.

Another mile, another two. Three more because Noah is stubborn like that. They pull over for some tosser driving up their arse with full beams on. Low cloud, rolling cold. And Brian tells Noah about the note and the nationalism. How they wiped his recorder and gave him a number. Noah listens to everything, foot still heavy.

Quiet again for a few minutes. Then Noah, eyes in his mirrors, under his breath:

Spectacle, that was.

What?

Spectacle. Operatic. It was like a Greek frigging tragedy.

Brian squeezes his fists. He turns his gaze sideways on Noah.

Who shot him, Noah?

Noah sighs. Huffs nearly. God knows, he says.

Why aren't you arsed?

Why all the questions, kidder? You seen one go down, you seen them all. Bastard had it coming probably.

Seemed harmless though. Harmless.

Noah shrugs.

Wrong place to put a foot wrong, then. Just makes you wonder –

Wonder what?

If that crap he spouted held a little water – I mean, the cameras caught it. Says to me they knew it were coming.

Brian shakes his head – he can't shake the image.

Things don't sit right. His stomach's in knots and his mouth's dry. His meat is throbbing.

Like a hit?

If you want to be a drama queen about it. Must've pissed off the wrong people someplace.

He spoke to me.

You said.

He stared at us.

Noah laughs.

You look a dreamboat. I would've too. Whole room did.

But things aren't right. The things Ian said – he saw through me, didn't he?

Mate. Come on. Paranoia is that. We get back, call Garland. We adapt. We got what we came for. Ian isn't arsed about you.

No? Well a card with his digits says he is. Says I'm involved. And I reckon you need to call Garland before home.

Get yourself a mobile, did you?

No, and I'm not saying –

So button it and chill out, right? I'll speak to Harry, see if his lot know owt. End of the day, a bloke got himself smoked – and shitty while that is, it isn't our business. Garland wants what we went and got. Pays me, gets your nouse and mine, and we go home. Job well done, cash down, etcetera. And you – you go back to vegetating with your soldiers on telly, pockets full, nose fuller.

And Ian?

What about Ian? Forget about bloody Ian. Buttered you up a treat for a Billy-bullshitter, didn't he? Bin that business card too. Jokers and cranks, all of them. Won't do anything for you, Bri. I promise. Small fry, aren't they? Yorkshire ponces.

Brian sniffs. Feels that drip. His guts still tightening and squeezing.

It felt like news, though, Brian says. Like something bigger happening. Them lads and their rifles on the way up there –

Rhetoric always does you daft bastard. Maybe I were wrong bringing you out this way. But see, this just says there's a heart under that bonnet, doesn't it? I were wrong about them and all – all that crap about the future of our fair city. Simple as. Silly kids with grand plans. Can say what we're all thinking about this country but no substance after that. Needs more syrup, that kind of plotting. Same revolutionary shite you'll get in any pub – any white van ten years back. A shade of piss-poor terrorism I should've seen through.

Only they shot somebody, Brian says. We saw it. They just bloody shot somebody. That's bloody substance. They've got people watching them – council didn't raid that auditorium, did it? And they shot somebody dead.

They did, son. They did –

And now we're going home. Just like that.

Home to thrones in baths. Bunkers and drug labs.

Just remember, Noah says. As many drugs as you like.

But there's a problem with Noah's old car. It's not having it. The car's falling to bits in the wind and rain. And there, by the carcass of a phonebox, on the lips of a hill, their metal husk flashing between the ribs of the moors, the second headlamp gives in – it flickers out.

Darkness. Old-school, horror-book dark. From white cats' eyes to nothing out front – only red dots from far-away vehicles in the mirrors.

Noah swears. Noah keeps on swearing. He punches the wheel.

This bastard car, he says. This bastard, bastard car.

This bastard car that stops in a lay-by – stops sharp and savage. This bastard car getting panel-beaten under so much rain. The endless static. Mother Nature's own signal and noise.

Noah whips his seatbelt off since it wasn't fastened properly. It rolls away and slaps the plastic.

No worries, he goes, got a spare in the toolbox.

You're a real handyman, says Brian.

Noah dips under the steering column, pops the bonnet after struggling with the release catch.

Bloody thing, he says, the bonnet wobbling. To Brian: Stay put and wrap up while I sort it.

Brian nods, still catching breath.

Now, Noah's round the back with the boot up, rummaging in his tools. A wet wind cuts through the car.

Brian takes this chance to fish out a baggie. He dips his front-door key in the sniff and back to his nose.

The boys are in their lay-by. Their lay-by on the hill.

Noah, he's clicking the light on and off, concentrating. The new bulb works, but only just. A piss-weak yellow beam catching reflective signs ahead.

You're not still sulking, he says to Brian.

Eh?

Not sulking, are you?

No, says Brian, eyes rolling. But a man was shot. All that –

Noah tosses Brian his notepad. You've seen worse, I promise. Bigger fish, anyway. Just shut up for five and have a gander in there.

What for?

A library of bullshit is what.

Brian looks. The reluctant kind of looking. He leafs absently through these sketches that Noah made in the auditorium. Noah's sketches with crosses through. Question marks next to circles.

Them prats yapping on up there, giving it all that, says Noah. Mostly plant hire companies aren't they? These are old JCB parts, never you mind precision engineered – there's nowt in any of it. Any of it! Chatting shit, them lying bastards were. Sheep-shagging bastards. You could crap out half what they're saying they can build. Go on, look.

I just think we need to get off, says Brian. Get home –

Look at this one, Noah tells him, ignoring him, pulling Brian back a few pages. Make sense of that, you'll get a biscuit.

Brian guesses it's meant to be a half-track from the sketch. Some sort of truck cab converted to manage bigger loads without a trailer. Bigger loads like field guns, maybe. Saves on diesel that way, or so say the notes.

Noah breathes through his nose. He fingers the page.

Half these joints couldn't bear loads, he says. And this idea's from a respected engineering firm, apparently. Doesn't add up.

No? says Brian.

No, goes Noah. I mean maybe there is something else going on there. But that doesn't matter to us: Garland's going to lay eggs when he finds out half his competition don't have a bloody clue what they're on about.

So why did we bother?

Same reasons anybody bothers with anything. The cash and the fanny.

But you didn't hear him, Brian says. It's like he's planning a coup.

Pulling out with one light. You look left and you look right. Careful though: with one light down when it's this dark, you'll look like a motorbike from a distance.

Half a fag goes out the window. Movement. Brakes –

Stop. From the right, two speeding cars shear an edge off the nearest corner. They kiss the apex and shift down for the hill in front, the second so close it's a shadow of the first. Spray goes everywhere. Black cars, their tyres bobbling along the cats' eyes.

Behind them, another car, its lights out – erratic on the centre line – follows. This car's arse-end waggles on the exit and accelerates hard. Doesn't take much to work out it's in pursuit.

Noah looks at Brian. Out through the wet glass.

Dickheads, he says, shaking his head. Get cracking, shall we?

One light, Brian thinks.

And as they climb another incline, rain turns to hail turns to snow. Liquid goes to solid in a hundred metres or less. Not surprising, not this high, not in these hills, but you feel it. You'd say, *Rough out.*

Brian watches the wipers at full pelt. Noah's hard over the wheel, his length making him into a kind of tight curly-cuh.

Hard hills, these, for an old man of a car. To get anywhere, and especially up the hills, you need the momentum first. It's momentum they don't have much of.

Then at the top, eventually, a left, a right, and the lads – just as they're yawning – see the red together.

The red cuts through the sleet, turns it into a cloud. Orange on, orange off. Bright against the slate and the water – actually it's bright red everywhere you look. The two of them are so tired and wired in this red light and smoke.

Noah slows. Noah swallows. Nobody's laughing now. There's none of that shining wit now. The smell hits then, clutch smoke.

84

There's a smell and the sound of gears still engaged. Of unconscious feet jammed on accelerators.

Closer, where it's louder, where the rain seems wetter, they see a hole in the wall just by there. Dry stone walling punched clean through and blasted out. The car down there on its nose, tail lights up, hazards on. Bits all over; tempered glass winking from the gravel.

Screaming, the vehicle is. Squealing – revving and revving and revving.

Noah and Brian edge past. They crawl past. Rubberneckers them both – the smoke thick and given shape by the red light.

Poor bastard, says Noah. Not a place to park is that.

Shit, says Brian, noticing at last –

A purple Transit. You can tell in spite of the night.

So Noah just belts it. Drives on hard.

No more of your paranoia trips, Brian, he says. No – *shh* – don't say a frigging word.

Brian doesn't believe it. Brian is stunned.

We can't leave it like that, he says. That's just happened. Them two cars – we can't be leaving it.

Noah's car nudges forty. Forty-five.

One thing for me, Brian pleads.

Noah's very quiet.

Noah?

Old buddy, old pal.

Noah, you prick. I just had to make out like some bugger blew my leg off in Afghanistan. Had Yorkshire pricks poking guns in my face. Humiliated in a room without a view. Lost in all your big man shite, the one-up-manship and whatever the hell else. Saw some poor sod get shot, just so you had an easier ride. So you'll turn round and go look in that wreck. Least you can bloody do. One thing for me.

So Noah stands on the brake pedal; stops them on a penny. It makes the third time this evening.

Noah grabs Brian by the cheeks and shakes his face.

One more thing for you, he says, the spit stringing at the corner of his mouth. You're a bloody drip you are, son. Stop bleating and remember that if you open cans you eat the worms.

Brian does know. But that Transit, or a Transit just like it, has been everywhere. Waiting, parked, following him bloody everywhere.

Please, Brian says.

One thing for you, Noah says again.

There, high up in the sleet and under the slate, Noah cranks reverse. He crunches it; bloody mashes the car into gear he's that wound up. He sends the car backwards till the engine's good to burst. He lets the car go a few metres more and throws it into a sloppy J-turn. Movie-style; a belly-in-mouth manoeuvre, a clever-clever sort of stunt.

Round and straight and back towards the red air. The red air and the broken wall. The stalker van on its nose, rear doors tilted slightly towards Manchester.

One headlight to light the way on the A628. Not a single other way back.

On account of Brian's tail, Noah gets out on his tod. On his tod and back into the wasteland. He throws a tatty blue cagoule over his jacket – never one for style, of course, but a big fan of function. He bounces down the embankment to the broken van. Noah all bandy and agile through the slop, the mud, the grass. Around the stones scattered wide by the impact. This strong man so used to climbing buildings. So used to leaping up walls and glass and metal to paint his pictures.

The van's dug in hard. Really dented – a write-off, if we're honest. He bends down by the driver's door to look. Bends down, looks in, and falls backwards.

Brian waits in the car – patient, patient Brian. Patient Brian who can't mount kerbs or staircases. Patient Brian who can't stand firm. Patient Brian who waits endlessly for cheques and sex and proper legs.

Bang the horn if you need owt, Noah has told him. Just keep that bald bloody head of yours down – like a lighthouse, that is.

The red light turns off, the red sky gone with it. Through the rain, Brian hears metal pull over metal; something like door handles and sliding fixtures. The traffic far away. The rain over glass. This dark and stormy night. Brian's face streaming with watery shadows in the passenger seat.

Our Brian with a wet finger in the bag of sniff – a naughty sherbet dip to blunt it all.

Two, three, four, five minutes tick by on the analogue. He gets to feeling alone.

Another five notches on the clock, and Noah crests the embankment, his head cowed against the weather. He rounds his wrecked car and opens the boot. Silent even there. It's odd for him, this man of so many words.

Noah bundles himself into the car, soaked through – and not just with rain. Noah's sweating hard, coughing.

He starts the car and rams the heaters to full whack.

He stinks of vomit.

What's going on? says Brian.

Nothing. Just let me think.

The smell gets everywhere.

What was it?

Shut up!

Noah pulls away, over-revving, stuck in first till Brian near as changes up himself.

Brian gags.

Tell me, Noah.

So Noah does. Noah just says it flat –

Head was off, wasn't it. Wet bits all over the cab. Picture of some little girl stuck to the windscreen.

The prickling skin, the goosebumps, the water in your eyes.

Driving back fast. Hanging corners tight. The Beetham memorial column soon tearing the sky – Manchester on fire with lights in the basin below as they bear down on dead reservoirs and damned villages.

Who was it?

Your man. That Colin.

And none of this will end well.

8.

Home again, where no hearts live.

There were a thousand locks before his chair – before a bath, maybe a tug. Certainly a joint. Anything to get himself off to sleep.

But first, before any kind of bath, he sits. Sits and sweats; back with the screens and their dead pixels. Back in his castle while the rain comes sideways. Getting on now as well, isn't it. A long night it's been, stretching itself longer now. Monday in the early hours. Let's turn on the telly, see who or what's been bombed, and where.

He skins up a last joint. It's to help him take stock and kill the last hour. Something mindless like that. Food if he can be bothered – dial L for Lamb – though he's not really hungry owing to the dread. Maybe telly if he can find the remote. Maybe more of these soldiers at war if he can stomach it.

Maybe nothing. Maybe a noose on the stairlift –

It all drifts. Time slipping, him with it. Thoughts of the staring man, head in bits, wet bits and chunky bits. That shot – the auditorium as it erupts. The feeling you can't go back and switch yourself off. The regret he didn't say no. That he said anything at all.

Thoughts then of Noah's last commandment. Noah who smelled like sick in the car, and who warned Brian to stay in for the next morning.

Be there, he'd said. We sort this then.

What's to sort?

Sort this mess.

What's to sort?

Straighten our stories.

Noah!

Brian swears again. Brian back with his monitors, gasping for a smoke. He flicks his monitors on and presses rewind. He kicks back. Traces an imaginary line between the corners of the ceiling. The feed from the day runs backwards on the left screen, the right screen pulling live pictures in but not recording.

In the corner, on now, the telly blares about its dead soldiers and bad debt.

Brian concentrates on the monitors as best he can. Divert the gaze and it's easier to forget. A good time to concern yourself with things you might've missed.

And on that screen the odd cars pass and people stutter along. Nothing untoward, in structure or in form. It's easy to spot the odd moments, these days. Even with the recording going backwards, he can tell after so much practising; after all these years of staring and waiting. Because at this speed, six times standard playback, and even though it's running backwards, it's the lighting that talks. Because in 2018, in this time after postmen, your front gates rarely swing.

The facts: if you see the lighting change, it's your gates open. That's when you pause. When nine times out of ten some smackhead comes up the path to buzz the doors and run their mouth. When you ask him to read the stickers and the warnings. When he turns and goes.

But no, nothing.

Just Colin. Colin. Colin. Colin. Like that.

Colin, Colin – Colin. The dead stranger staring for always.

90

Brian's stomach tightens. He's panicking and stoned. A real bad crowd, a right bad shower he's met tonight. And you, Brian, looking at half a reflection in the monitor – you with this meat for legs with no sea in sight. This was you as well. Opportunities like getting off your wide, widening arse. Buttered you up, didn't they – buttered you up and stuck a sharp one in you.

Back home, here, panicking at the core of his world, safe behind the cameras and the deadbolts. And then, an idea:

He has a way to survive this. A way through. The old way. The way he knows better than any other.

He still has hair while there's none on his head.

Brian laughs. Brian gets the scissors out. He grabs a spare elastic band for tradition's sake. A bit of spit to keep it neat.

Brian has other hair. Brian undoes his belt.

Brian has the broken sleep of a troubled man. Never the calm of the just. But the bad night's sleeping you can get used to. Some dreams, you can't.

That same damn dream – the sweat and the sounds. Apples and worms; taut cables and cars. Post-its, post-its, poems. Half a man parked in a car by the lamp post.

Setting off hard –

And then a woman. A woman looking down from a watchtower. A watchtower in a nest of sharpline. A spotlight turned across a field.

White out –

The sea, then. The shore. The watchtower a lighthouse now, somebody shouting through a megaphone:

You're too close to the shore, Brian! Come back!

Somebody rustling closer. Whispers and peace.

Sitting on a knee, a knee by the sea, bobbing. Soft hands in curly hair. The same voice:

91

You're useless. Worthless. Wish you'd never bloody happened. A deviation. Aberration.

Whispering, rocking gently.

You've ruined everything. My little –

White.

Fade up to a city across the water. A skyline of old Mancunian towers, some buckled.

The morning comes and the speakers sing – the tannoy ringing in this carcass of a house.

Ding dong.

It's still Monday.

A visitor, sir, the tannoy says.

Three times the tannoy says that, each a little slower than the last. It isn't a dynamic system, though – nothing so flash. The messages are recorded; speakers are wired to the entry buttons and really you'll only ever hear that one message.

A visitor, sir.

Brian with light through his lashes. A hand over rough stubble on his chin and fod.

Ding. Dong.

All.

Days.

The.

Same.

Brian swears and pulls the fallen blanket around him. Still wearing his smart trousers – still stained and scuffed with that moorland grit.

He turns the monitors on for a look. The entrance cameras burn white – still set to IR. He switches this, prods at that. Mutters stuff.

Then into the link microphone: Who's there?

Presently the man comes together on his screen. He

has floppy hair and smashed-glass teeth – this bloke grinning up at the cameras like a moron. The epaulettes say official business, council most likely. Bloody pissing down outside. Rain on the tarmac comes across the speakers like hard static.

Name's Kenneth, Mr –

Kenneth?

From the North West Ambulance Trust.

Day we on?

Um, Monday sir. You've a skin appointment with Dr Abbas at the CHU. Ten AM.

Sorry?

My name's Kenneth, Brian. I'm with the North West Ambulance Trust.

I'm not in, says Brian. He clicks to wide-angle outside. Kenneth's big old pig sitting there, turning over. This one's a tracked field cart with a red cross and a red crescent up its side. Really heavy weather. Probably the wettest in weeks.

Sir –

I told you bastards I don't speak to any of you 'cept Diane, and she's the sharpest pain in my arsehole as it is. Take me for a bloody mug?

Sir –

Plus I don't recall any appointments, and if I had any, Diane would've showed up first.

But sir, I –

Buzz off, will you? Take that bastard uniform and your tractor and hop it.

Diane Kadam has been deported, Brian.

You what?

Seems her husband was funding ideals and nasty ideas the council don't tolerate.

Brian stares –

I'm your case officer now.

–

Monday, bloody Monday.

The pig's ride falls on the wrong side of smooth. Brian sits up front, Kenneth driving. In the back, a tin rolls from top to tail, sticking on old spilt liquids or pinging off the seat fixtures when they hang a sharp corner.

These tractors do nowt for your piles, Brian says. Nowt in it for any of us. Gets right on my tits. Can't smoke. Can't eat. Probably can't soil yourself in here case the council cries foul. And you're all calling this a bloody ambulance now, are you?

Two miles in, and Kenneth's patient smile is wearing thin.

Big boys don't cry, Kenneth says. These half-tracks did their time when we needed them – seems a waste to give up on the old dears now.

Just saying, goes Brian. Mess they've made of our roads.

Rivers of blood need their mops, Brian.

You'd know, would you?

I saw my share.

Well, like I meant it. Just saying.

If you don't like it, you could join the emigrants and shoot east for the warm.

That right? And get myself cancers for bothering?

Just an idea wasn't it. If it's bad skin you've got –

Don't make assumptions. You don't get out of here on my kind of meal ticket. No job. No work in this place anyway. Specially not for cripples.

Moan a lot for someone who's so looked after, don't you? Used to have pubs open all day for people like you.

94

What the hell do you know about me or what I think?

Just think it can't be much worse with the sun on your back is all. Damp gets you in the chest, doesn't it?

Brian thinks of home. The meat for legs and the chances lost. His Thursdays without Diane –

Life without Diane – without that brolly shaken up his wall. Back to bare bulbs and tinnies for breakfast –

The rest of his life with this tail for a bottom half.

Everything gets me in the chest, Brian says, with his eyes filling. Everything.

He looks down at the meat. At the absolute principals of cause and effect. He sniffs.

Now you want a nice conversation, Ken, you let a bastard like me smoke out your windows.

But Kenneth shakes his head. Eyes front. Not on your nelly, sunshine. Not by the hairs on my chinny-chin-chin.

Then get me in this doctor's face and on my way.

In the chest.

Ashton, anyway. They get there after a fashion.

Ashton is the town that turned into the city's main market district after what they did to Salford. It's deathly quiet except on Tuesdays, Thursdays and Saturdays, when the buses roll in and the day's best deals roll out. Ashton's the town that rose from a fire that gutted everything in 2004. Ashton, a monument to the city and the way it swallows up the past – the way it grows outwards or simply makes everything else grow in.

The fire was the best thing that happened, the locals might tell you. Because proper markets come far and between.

The sheen's off it now, course. The enamel is cracked. They threw the Metrolink through here before they binned the timetables and then the trams, and now when you pass the decaying station you kind of hold your breath – it's an essay on the council's messy policies in very few words. Suburban Manchester left to the worms. The main railway into town where the worst kind of people do their business – usually Wilber gangs bartering over people they've caught that week. The brothels across the road doing a fine trade.

Brian and Kenneth, they cross a roundabout by a shattered dual carriageway. A gentle incline and overgrown weeds roll out in front. They pass through a gated checkzone with cameras for sides, and into the bays where the CHU has a sign to go with the acronym. CONSOLIDATED HEALTHCARE UNIT, it says. 500-point words down the side of the main office. Signwritten by amateurs who couldn't afford the neon.

In the quiet, in Kenneth's pig, Brian's preoccupied with Noah and Colin and death. The calls and the sorting. Still stuck in yesterday – in last night. Sick as a parrot because he's meant to be home, isn't he. Meant to be waiting for the door and the skinny man fresh from his bunker. More drugs. Success stories and cash. Rewards. Garland happy. A bit of talk about the man they saw – Colin, who got shot twice in a night. Whose face came off in his cabin –

Unloaded, refolded. Brian, the origami man, back in the chair. The lumpiest man you ever saw.

And Kenneth wheels him to the entrance, whistling some tune or other. About all you'll hear of music since nobody has the disposable income to afford frivolities like instruments. With the internet off, it's pretty hard to listen to anything, either.

Brian, well he makes out like enough is enough. Kenneth says to him, I can wait, or you can grab a train back and brave them Wilbers. 'Cept there aren't any trains to-day, so actually it's best you're nice.

It's not a new building – hardly a building at all if you're pedantic – but for a temporary structure it's obviously been round a while. Close enough to the satellite towns to the east of Manchester, and not Stockport, which burnt for six savage months at the height of the riots. Course, there's the odd scorch mark you can't paint over. Bits of it coloured with big stains; bits where the glue's gone and panels are flapping about. Many ramps – ramps stapled over steps owing to some kind of rehabilitation programme for the amount of smashed infantrymen coming home from the fronts.

When they go inside and see the faces, they both re-member Ashton CHU is also the borough sex clinic.

Kenneth nudges Brian. He opens his hand and rubs his thumb and forefinger together.

Give, he says.

So on account of sex, this place is where latent guilt and responsibility meet – where people of all years and no obvious symptoms collide.

Brian's been sitting here five minutes having told the smug receptionist his name. On account of sex they tell you it's all anonymous, but the blushing from all cor-ners says more than a surname ever would, and anyway, you'll usually see half these people on the bus ride in.

They breeze about him in reception. People coming, going, big arguments between couples trying to keep it all so quiet. A lot of tears before noon. And all about, they're wondering how to tell the boyfriends and the partners; the girlfriends, the wives and the mistresses.

All accepting that if you put private things in other

people's private places, you're accountable.

This tall lad springs from the double-doors, jolting the whole reception room. He nods to a few more behind Brian. He's a right one, this bloke is.

Haven't even got a name for what I've got! he shouts.

Shouting loud and proud in this place where they put Latin names to faces. Patients and outpatients.

A pretty nurse turns out. Brian, please, she says.

And through.

Dr Abbas is a heavy man with thin wrists. He wears a gold watch and has a tongue like gristle. He holds one knee over the other; taps a pen just behind his ear. He's reading notes off a tablet – pretending he's on with doctorly pursuits in this fully barren surgery.

Good morning, Brian, he says, glancing up the once.

Hello.

And how've we been?

Aye, all right. Not bad.

Well that's – ahh, one moment.

Brian's chair creaks.

Dr Abbas puts his pen down.

Right. Yes. Where were we? Oh, I like your new haircut.

Cheers.

So. I understand you saw Diane Thursday.

Yes.

Dr Abbas claps his hands. Pretends to look arsed. And you understand she won't be with the unit anymore?

Weather the storm – that's what Brian thinks.

Yes, he says.

Okay. Terrible circumstances actually. But it's not for me to comment. And, well, so you know, we're working out a contingency. It may be the case we don't visit you this Thursday. Will you have enough food?

Brian nods. Expect I'll manage. It's the beer I worry about.

Dr Abbas smiles and puts down his tablet. He pushes his glasses on. Stands to pull a good metre of sterile paper over his bed. For all the cuts and all the hassle, they've harped on enough to guarantee a clean backside.

Good, he says. Very good.

Now Dr Abbas invites Brian to sit up on the paper and the bed.

How've your legs been?

Brian moves close and lifts himself from the chair. Unsteady, unwieldy. A little indignant. Meat, not legs – and never forget it.

The same they've always been, says Brian. You look after your own.

Well, if you'd just remove your trousers and we can take a look.

Funny how you don't call these a trouser, Brian says.

Brian sits there with trousers pulled down to his ankles.

That'll do, Brian.

Dr Abbas begins to pick and prod. Gentle over new scabs and old scars. Tracing round the blotches. By the knee, Brian takes a sharp breath; has to stop short of a yelp.

You're picking at this too often, my friend. It is worsening. Are you moisturising? Are you using the cream we gave you?

Brian thinks, You don't have to moisturise scales. It's the sea they want. But let them grow you'll be crucified.

Brian nods. Brian is fine and upstanding. Brian says, Course I'm bloody moisturising.

Then we'd better think about admitting you again. At the very least to try phototherapy. We did say –

No.

You know you leave us little choice when you choose to ignore your health. Your condition causes complications as it is.

My condition's perfectly natural, says Brian.

Dr Abbas frowns. He says something about genetic screening. Gene therapy. Then, when he sees Brian's face, he says, Of course. But Brian, you must understand my concerns. You are a rarity, for certain. But you are not untreatable. Not invincible –

I get by, though.

Well, I'd like you to consider counselling again.

Brian laughs. To tell me what? About my mother and her politics? What a demic I am?

No. To help.

Don't need it. All right for dark rooms, me. Feel a right dick talking with folk you don't know from Adam.

That's fine, Brian. I'm simply suggesting –

Well don't. I don't need people telling me how to deal with these wheels or otherwise.

Dr Abbas breathes heavy. He says, I'd also like to take a small blood sample.

Fine.

Dr Abbas leans away.

And if and when we're done, you could urinate in this cup, and cover it with this kitchen towel. Toilet's through there, down that corridor. Third on the right.

Think I'm riddled as well? says Brian. Think you'll meet your next appointment if you send me off down there doing that?

Dr Abbas chuckles. No, perhaps not. But it's standard now. I have to update the central records. Still, from the looks of that arm I'll struggle to find a vein.

And Dr Abbas isn't wrong. He has to prick Brian four times till it comes. Plenty out, thick and good.

Oh look, the doctor says, a beam spreading across his chops. It's starting to bruise already.

There's something on the door step. A bloody gnome on first looks.

By the second, by the time he's closer, he sees it's a black dog wrapped in gold foil. Quick glances left and right like he's on telly being filmed for a hard-boiled detective show.

Closer again, it becomes Anubis in six inches – Anubis in wood, hand-painted, and strikingly done.

Brian leans and scoops, baffled. Weighs it – damn weighty for wood – and strokes the dog nose, the lines in the head-dress. Certainly he's meant to find it.

A look around. The empty street. The ash-grey road. A moment to figure; to think and connive.

Brian chucks Anubis in his lap, racks the locks and bowls inside – inside with the sweet smell of old weed and milk on the turn. Home to the stains and all those empty tins. The grooves in his lino and black lines over floors.

Then, he puts Anubis on the side near the bibles. Where crap like that always ends up. Wonders if it's a wind up; a warning or worse. All the while holding the statue's dead gaze, taking the time to pick his nose. See our Brian knows all about Anubis, the books he's read. Books he's read and notes he's made.

Anubis stares back, blanking all.

Pal, you're a paranoid man. You have cameras on your house – you know where to check.

So Brian kicks his monitor bank and flicks the telly on. Brian with a pen and a pad. In his chair, under that bulb.

This, this excites him and it freaks him out. The way mystery does a lot for imagination. This message in wood. And leastways it's something to qualify doing nothing. Let's play hard-boiled detective after all. Find a happy ending – his happy-ever-after. Something to help forget the day before. Something over Noah since Noah can bloody well wait.

And he's found half a jay in the glass ashtray. Enough to pique a sober morning.

Blazing up, leaning forward, winding back the dial that makes for fizzy screens and wonky lines. Looking for that light – the gate opening.

Some bastard did it. Some bastard's made the effort.

Ten minutes turns out nothing. Three hours scanned. Past early morning and on to night. Back again – and back again.

He sees himself lock and leave. Sees Kenneth up close and talking fast – Kenneth reversing down his drive and into the pig. The pig tracking backwards, bellowing diesel smoke.

Pause. Play. Rewind. The same scenes the right way round. The same scenes ten times over. The telly a dead noise in the background.

Brian blows smoke and pens his pad. Waits and waits. Then:

The gate. The wrought iron gate teased out. A fast shadow on the concrete.

Two eyes and a mouth wreathed in black. The back of a head. Three frames, chopped up and glaring.

He thinks it out. Feels his heart go, his belly gone heavy –

Going deeper into this, where the lights start winking out. The cold sweats starting, your vision purpling at the edges.

His stomach lurches.

So write it down, then, you bloody idiot –

Yorkshire bastards.

Yorkshire bastards who weren't coming in, but going out.

Time for Noah now, with the morning done. Dirty men in his dirty den – sick feelings getting stronger by turns. But the phone's still missing. The phone he threw. And the answerphone blinks sixteen; sixteen messages from then till now.

Brian. You have sixteen new messages.

He presses play and settles back from the bare mantle. His eyes wide.

Take a grip; take the hit. Sixteen bastard messages from then till now.

One:

Wakey wakey, Brian. Shit's gone off. My Cherry's been had off. Bastard gone! Two lads in a tow truck wearing hi-vis, in two minutes. Un-fucking-believable. We need to talk about last night. Something – shit. Harry's on the other line. Call me back.

Two:

Brian. Me again. Look – I pulled something out of his van. It's . . . it's incredible. You need to see it. Pick up, call me. Pulling a few favours with the car now. Try you again in five.

Three:

Where are you? Answer the phone you bumbling fool. My car's been taxed by a bunch of gits in hi-vis jackets!

Four:

Getting on for half past now. We're running out of time. I need –

Five:

Answer your bloody phone, pal. Please. Don't have all morning and nor do you.

Six:

Brian. Noah again. Got a job on this afternoon now, so we need to sort you out with a joe and get you over this way. Harry's got me painting canal bridges phos-pink for a pretty penny, so I'll need to be seeing you in the next hour –

Seven:

The hell you playing at, son? Get in touch.

Eight:

Fuck's sakes –

Nine:

Brian? You there?

Ten:

Brian. Things are changing already. You see it outside first, then right down to your pores. Give us a bell. Don't want to mither you like this all bloody day.

Eleven:

Taking the piss, aren't you pal? Well here's a thing. You're on the wrong side of this fence. Everyone is. Garland too.

Twelve:

Should've started worrying the fourth time you had me on this bastard machine. Shape up and ship out. Got it? Just ring when you get this.

Thirteen:

Only me. Got your gear and cash here, fella. Grateful?

Fourteen:

It only scares you at first, Brian. Only first time. Then you take it and hold it dear; hold it close and sniff it hard. I don't know what's happening but –

Fifteen:

I said I'd tell you a story while we wait for you to pull

that fat arse out of sleep. Well here's a story. Heard of Ascension Island, haven't you son? Maybe not. Military base, basically, though pretends not to be. Seen a lot of war; a lot of war and a lot of suits. Out on the way to the Antarctic circle and those kind of places. Anyway, when we garrisoned Ascension Island – us British I mean, the Navy, late 1700s or early 1800s or whenever that was. Well whenever it was, we took all these bloody ponies with us. Good for ferrying crap about, aren't they? Pulling this and that. But see when you've lit candles, you don't need the match anymore, so likewise when we've got our homes and our walls and our prisons built, we leave the buggers out in the cold. Just like that, pretty things out there with the flowers. So years go on like they do, and eventually, well, they go wild these ponies. But they don't change. Don't change 'cause when you've got a fondness for nice plants, you'll like a bit of posh garden. A pony's a pony, and a nice English garden out on an island in the Atlantic is still a nice little garden. So they piss off the locals, don't they. Munching away on flowers and shrubs. A man's garden is his moat, right? But instead of blasting their heads clean out like you'd think, the settlers got clever. Installed a ton of cattle grids. Big iron things that go red in three years, yeah, that'll work. And it did, actually. For a bit. Stopped 'em coming in. And yet, after a while, the plants start getting munched on and trampled again. Nobody can work it out. But the ponies know. They know. Put a cattle grid between a pony and his scran, he'll start to think. He'll start to plot. So they camp out, these locals. And they find out that these ponies, these clever bloody ponies, well they've learned to roll over cattle grids haven't they?

Sixteen:

Are you sleeping, Brian? Dreaming of tin soldiers out

105

there on the fields? You know, they bury you faster in hot countries.

Next news, the phone rings; sends Brian half a metre backwards.

Owing to his arm, Brian can't answer. Brian can't take his calls. Won't get up the stairlift in time to catch the other.

After the tone, please record your message –

This happening right now. Noah on the blower after what sounds like a full night on the lash.

You have a new message.

Seventeen:

It's about format, Brian. Because God has made us to adapt. To become butterflies. And I'll fly, Brian. I'll wait till my change comes. He's made me a butterfly.

It's light out but getting darker inside. The fractal world, falling through his windows into shapes that repeat bigger shapes before splitting into their own.

Early afternoon Monday in the arsehole of the world. A small war to list among the others.

Brian thinks free and loose. Hard thoughts. Fast ones, churned ones. Thoughts about caving; calling the police – the old way to make a scene. Thoughts about nobody liking a grass round this way. The convenient way people can turn an eye. Thoughts about how things that happen in the corners of dark rooms, and stay in the corners. Thoughts about the strings coming down from men on the hills – men coming into his house.

Time for changing. Time for rolling. Time for half a ton of coke blasted up both bloody nostrils. To move into the grey mess, the mush of a high, and learn for himself. To sort out the night gone before.

Brian turns off the lights. Sits in this pastel afternoon.

What he assumes: Noah has lost his marbles. Lost the

plot. Off his tits on something or other. Not slept; wired, he doesn't know. He isn't all there, though – not from any angle. All this deranged talk, this bluster. Seventeen messages and barely three that made sense. This box he's on about – what box?

What he knows: No cops. No convenience. A dirty wood for this dirty world.

Anubis watches.

And Brian sets off for the stair lift. A sorry man dragging himself along by hand and wheel. Hand over wheels – the bent spokes still causing a bit of a dip every other rotation.

9.

For sure, Tariq sounds shorter down a phone. He's driving, shouting. Doesn't remember Brian on first hellos, either. Stands to reason when you think of all those faces in the back; harder still owing to the wind through his windows.

Brian, Brian's upstairs with Tariq's business card shaking in his hand. This new pastime of fear and panic, his red eyes rolling over his archives. His throat lumping out –

Salaam aleikum.

It clicks for Tariq the third time Brian says his name.

Hang on. That guy outside the Cat Flap?

Yeah, goes Brian.

Quality mate! As if you found my digits, state you were in. How's it going?

Not bad, aye.

And how's that head?

All right, yeah.

On the bed, an overnight bag for the man who won't often wash. A brown-bristled toothbrush for emergencies – like for when he pulls, ha, ha. A bag of joints he already built. Moisturisers sitting on the shelves, out of date, veneered with dust. Those old scales twitching.

Good hangover I'll bet, shouts Tariq over road noise. Looked a right good night fella. You a full-time hobbyist?

The idea makes Brian gag.

Hang about, says Brian. Are you on a mobile?

No –

Then – then how?

Council network. Got a redirect for my CB.

Isn't that dodgy?

Tariq laughs.

What you after anyway?

You ever run daytime drops?

Pause. Then: I'm not even meant to be out now, so not really.

Always talking to men with cars, our Brian. Cars and agendas. Him and every last bastard on wheels.

So you do.

Depends doesn't it, says Tariq. Easier to get spotted. Won't see me in a white-man mask, mind, but them gantry-cams just love my number plates. Where we talking? I mean, can it wait till the sun's in?

In and out. It's the hell-run. I've got the cash – it's an emergency.

Hmm. Time you thinking?

About ten minutes ago.

To where was it again?

Shoe-shop in town. Inner Sole.

Right. Right. Well, I'll tell you what. Give me an hour. On my way to Wigan at the minute. You've heard about Birmingham, yeah?

No – what about it? An hour –

An hour-ish, yeah.

What's happened in Birmingham?

Kicked off big time my friend. Local lads running their mouths saying some brothers raped a young blonde. Solihull. All the local skinheads are on a promise, so it's not a time for my type to fanny about in the sunshine.

Jesus –

I don't believe it, pal. Grade-A smear. People make this crap up. Probably just another game for the truthers. But I'm shipping a party of brothers from Wigan to Piccadilly. Defence of the realm and all. Brum'll be on fire in a few hours they're saying. Cars getting turned over and roads blocked already – the King's troops on town lines as well. Got to get the lads down there to help, don't you? It's all over central radio.

Brian looks at his Olympic flag out in the hall. He remembers a lot of things.

You support them?

You what?

Do you support these lads?

Think I'd ferry white boys around if I did? You know the difference between a Muslim and these dickheads calling themselves Muslims, don't you mate? God's not always great, Brian. Of course he isn't. But a man's got kids to feed. We all do. And sometimes, skin-heads need teaching in the only language they understand.

I don't get what you –

Just saying that these boys I'm shifting aren't terrorists or rapists or thugs. They're going to stop knee-jerk pillocks from burning mosques. 'Cause tomorrow it'll get like it always is. The pigs out in their pigs for old times' sakes. Fire and brimstone and all that. And besides, I say it's the bloody chinks you want to keep an eye on – beware the red peril and that.

Maybe, says Brian.

I were joking fella.

I said, maybe.

Look, I'm going to go pal – doing my box in this. Think I've got your road saved in the old mind-map. Be seeing you in a bit.

110

I'll be out the front.
You won't miss me.

Tariq wasn't wrong. Tariq brought his very own community care bus. That old peculiar. *Your transport company* up the side. Tariq, with a grin, leaning on the air horn.

And Brian's in his yard, bent double by default, but creased into quarters he's laughing so hard.

And Tariq, hanging out of the window, laughs back.

The bus, oh, it's one of those friend-of-a-friend jobs. A pal with the right links; the right favours to pull. Ex-riot, ex-council, taxi. It's running red diesel but apart from that . . .

And Tariq says, Well what good's a pair of us when these old cans hold a team? The right way to roll around a curfew, this bad boy.

And a safe way to run Hyde Road – hell road – into town.

You only tip a joe if he got you there faster than the guy before. It's a new sort of etiquette now they say the oil's all but done.

Brian tips Tariq double and change. Tariq looks perplexed. Brian feels good. Brian goes, You've been a love.

So Tariq salutes him.

Some other time, bud, he says. And brother, you best take care now.

Brian's on the pavement, Tariq in the bus. The pair of them outside Inner Sole like they're waiting for the world to stop spinning. The red bricks all around; the tallest towers of Manchester clutching for space; the cracked pavements split with roots, the cracked pavements missing low kerbs.

Tariq winks and pulls away; nine gears to grind

through before he's moving proper. He pips at fifty yards, waves his hand out the window, and takes a left.

Brian holds his fortunes behind him. Noah's shop some big square magnet with the door swung fully open. The sign says closed.

It starts to rain. The inverted sea coming from the grey beyond. And Brian badly wants to sack this off. He gets some sense of loyalty dividing; friends falling into different orbits. Those ships in the night. He hates how much he cares.

He falls into the breach. He falls into all kinds of smell and mess.

Inside, the lights are strobing. Inner Sole is a bad scene going worse. Corner to corner, shoes carpet the shop. Single boots and safety-clamped slippers; too-white trainers and scuffed stilettos. A bad impression of Auschwitz. Noah's worst dreams spread out in separated pairs.

Most of the shelves are split as well. The backs kicked out of point-of-sale units with fat splinters to prove it. Benches lie on their backs, plates of ceiling tile swinging from wires. It's hard to move for the shoes.

The cash office is wrecked. A smashed strip bulb across the chair. A Medusa-coil of cables, their insides turned out. Everything smells like turpentine – like the plan for a big fire. By the desk, a carpet panel moved to expose a safe – and the safe hauled out and hacked in two. The threatening shapes in dark corners.

Face up, he finds a tick sheet with names and addresses all over it. Small text so you have to read closely. The prefixed names of doctors and council figures; PCs and Detective Superintendents.

Proof forever that Noah works for everyone.

Brian leaves the office. He wheels himself to the service lift. It screams open. He gets pitched into black, just a green backlight on the buttons, a vein of blue from the roof strip. The concertina doors rattle a dead tune for him.

In the basement, the bunker door is open a crack.

Brian sees a lot at once. Knows how none of this will end well.

Brian's hairs go up on their ends. Brian has found Noah. Noah is sitting on an office chair with his head between his knees; a line of sick from door to floor to feet. Noah, who's equidistant to all four walls and slap-bang under a single blacklight. Brian in the dark down in this lair, and boy does Brian feel sick.

Sick owing to the joggers round Noah's ankles, a death-sweet smell you can't mistake. That total loss of grace. And the black lights colour their skins a weird kind of brown, their hair purple besides. Noah's legs are made of hard muscles – cartoon lines like he's felt-tipped the muscle tone.

The generator drones in its heat enclosure. There's a bin by Noah's toes.

On the floor by the chair and the bin, Brian sees the wings. Noah has crafted wings in his bunker. Fancy ideas made facts with nets, chicken mesh, cable ties – sixteen feet round the edges, one on each side. Strips of blue tarpaulin in a pile, a sketched blueprint covered in notes.

The workbenches are turned over, more bookshelves torn out. Paper and globs of stuff Brian can't recognise. Chunks of wall and plaster.

Jesus, Noah –

Noah is still and breathing roughly.

Brian rolls close, pulling near. His ears scream with the sound of the sea.

Noah, says Brian. What have you done? Did someone come here?

Noah spits something thick on his feet. It slaps, shines. Noah starts convulsing from the hips up, the chair squeaking –

Noah laughing –

Jesus Christ, Brian says again.

The apocalypse as a man.

Noah. You're scaring the hell out of me.

Not dying, Noah says, head loose by his knees. He slurs the lot. Not dying, he says again, and raises a thin hand with fingernails halfway off. My chrysalis. Fly up our towers. Take that bastard Harry's work to the clouds.

Brian's too close to a strong smell. Sweet and racking, this smell – a stench you taste.

Brian is dizzy. Brian's throat is stuffed. Brian says, Come on . . . come on fella. Please. We're getting you some help.

And Noah sits up. Just sits up and grins. He pulls at his cheeks with his bleeding hands. His eyes are glued closed with something sticky.

Noah's face is ruined. Noah's lumpen face. There are fat sores running from his throat to his forehead. Red swellings – one closing his left eye, another for a cheek.

Tumours. Sarcomas.

Brian swears. Really cries blue murder in the room without a view. Never fair, is it. Not for our Brian. Brian has lived a curse; seen the done-for; found the damned.

The lumps are pulsing. These low, aching lumps, swelling and shrinking again –

Noah?

Not . . . anymore, says Noah. Don't you see? Adapt –

Brian sees Noah's teeth come loose while he talks.

Adapt –

Sees Noah's teeth loose and white in the rinse cycle of his mouth.

114

Noah, for Christ's sakes man.

Sees Noah chew his teeth, his gums opening –

Brian's stuck still. Struck dumb and dizzy. The burning in his throat. These tumours. What is it? he says. Noah! You daft bloody bastard – what've you done to your shop?

Noth-shing . . . elsh, says Noah, the blood down his chin. Pointing to these glinting wings he's made on the floor in his bunker.

Leaning and pulling out a box in a box from the bin, his frailty growing.

Thish – yours.

The city yawning for its butterfly.

The box skitters over the floor. It stops about halfway between them both. Brian swallows and swallows, can't get his throat to work.

Ish Colin's bosh, Noah tells him. You take ish and you hide ish. Don't open. Never –

Brian feels the room expanding and tearing in two; a crack running from the box and outways.

Noah laughs again. A right picture with his teeth all gone.

He looks happier than he ever has.

Two men followed Brian up the street. Brian was dazed. They asked what he was doing at Inner Sole. They had Yorkshire accents. Brian said he was buying drugs, same as anybody else.

Brian didn't put two-and-two together.

Brian just didn't care. Hardly knew where he was, or where he was going. His head swimming and his heart smashing out of his ribs.

Brian stole a lot of drugs on his way back out. It felt like a favour. It felt like he'd be the best person to look after them. He figured Noah didn't need to sell drugs anymore. It felt like Noah would appreciate the thought.

So Brian had about six grands' coke about his person and Colin's box in his lap. And these two men wanted to know if he'd heard about a job Noah had pulled a year or two ago. Painted a chimney up like a penis, they said. A condom advert for one of their competitors.

Brian did not have a clue. Brian didn't pay attention to adverts. Brian said, Adverts make you weak. Brian was trying to get home with a lot of drugs and some kind of artefact two men had now died for.

Because Noah was dead, wasn't he.

Because Noah was dead now. Had to be. It was obvious. Colin too. This box that Noah said was amazing but Brian should never open. And that's why Brian took all of Noah's stash. Because weed just wouldn't cut it on a night like this. And don't you know it.

So Brian offered this pair of men some coke, and one of them smiled and stuck his hand in the bag and licked it. He said, Hey, look. I'm like a Columbian police officer. Not racist if you think about it. And then he bought a couple of grams for quite a bit more than the usual price and disappeared off down the road, his partner in tow.

Brian breathed a sigh of relief and felt sick again. He felt very sick about Noah disintegrating. It'd been a bad afternoon. It'd been a bad start to the week.

And Brian did not see what to do, how to do it, where to do it or why he should have to. Because Brian had Colin's box now, and something had made Noah disintegrate, and usually Brian thinks a lot of causality.

So Brian went home with his box. Brian put the soldiers and the debt on.

Brian listened to news of Birmingham and rape and new riots.

Brian put the box on the table in his lounge.

Brian dumped Noah's stash by the front door.

Brian poured out a small baggie for safe-keeping and stuffed it in his pocket.

Brian started to cry.

Brian cut twelve lines of cocaine from the big bag and railed every single last one in a row, plus the crumbs, so that his nose bled and his brains were a disgusting muddle.

And he did not sleep till Tuesday. He didn't piss till Tuesday. And on Tuesday, he intended not to think at all.

10.

Wednesday, Brian starts to think. Starts to breathe quickly and starts to fret. Brian doesn't know if he dreamed it. It comes over him like guilt. The house is some sort of rotting womb between him and the world. Brian has a carbolic hangover.

Check the tapes, check the doors. His cycling life – a life on a loop – that he lives out inside.

This folded man on his way to being snapped. The fold at his waist becoming a score.

Ten minutes balanced over the toilet bowl, an hour in the bath. He uses a brillopad this morning. Brian with red legs and a brand new habit. It's some new way to assuage the guilt of inactivity. As he uses the skimmer to fish himself from the bath water and into the box, he knows everybody would think that. Just like he knows a man with proper legs would do more for a dying friend.

He seals the box of wet skin.

Brian makes a plan. Gets up and gets dressed in old wool and moth-bitten blankets. He'll make the time to ring Noah's shop. He'll take the time to confirm these nightmares. And he leaves the house and does it from a call box. He doesn't want people tracing his number. Brian thinking this is one way not to implicate himself. An alternative to finding an alibi on this street without neighbours. Plus it gets him out of the house. Out and away from the ghosts of a bad weekend.

Brian wedges himself in the call box; Colin's secret box in his lap. Last place you'd look – or maybe the first if you were a bastard. Adverts for the Cat Flap clinging on by their last corners of stick. Cassie and the other girls sucking their fingers for him. Good times guaranteed – for much less. Crude graffiti of dead soldiers and old-school NF slogans, always imaginative: PAKIS GO HOME; NO SURRENDER, but without the semi-colon.

Brian burns half his pot of emergency fifty pence pieces in the end. These coins he's collected for a long time – the fiscal section of his archive upstairs.

Our man in this fly-postered phone-box throwing his laughable savings at a dead number for an hour straight.

But Brian has to go home eventually. He lobs a last pair of fifties into the box and pecks out the number. The whispering static. The flat note.

Brian wishes mountains were molehills.

Back in the lounge with the telly on loud: bad news and bad debt and Birmingham bombed – those fresh riots already getting larger and worse. Another city burning. Bad feelings forming a sediment in his belly. Bad memories.

He's laid out Colin's box in front of him. Brian and this thing that's covered in dry blood. Sitting, falling, into the gravity well of this grim box. Six sides that took his friend and now this room. It's almost a whirlpool, our mermaid's adrift, his legs stuck together and his eyes closed. Four hours, five hours, face forward for the night. Just him and Birmingham on telly and Colin's box – a kind of singularity punching big chunks out of what he thinks is real and pulling him through. Brian in his stinking wool with that empty fridge nearby. Brian without his savings. Not on a wing, never with a prayer.

119

Anubis watches Brian from the top. Watches him watch the lines blur. Colin's box starting to talk to Brian about this and that.

Open me, it keeps saying. Go on. The box from the hills, from the van. Birmingham screaming as she burns –

The way the box doubles up when he loses focus. The way each edge whispers about heartache. The way his head swims – bursting, fit to pop.

The monsters are waiting beyond the lid. And the curiosity of change, of Noah's new face. Wondering if Colin's box did all that. If Noah meant all that. If this is why they shot Colin in his purple Transit. If this is why Noah came apart in the belly of his shoe shop. If this is the way to fix his breaking heart.

Thinking of the people on the insides of this stupid island, all of them wishing mountains were molehills. Because with every bead of sweat, Brian's losing salt and losing time.

And time isn't patient. Those hours keep passing –

Brian's so close to opening the box. As if the box is opening him. As if it's some kind of biblical temptation. And Brian is circling the plug hole. Brian's really in the shit; out of frying pans and into fires. The treasure and the reward. His head cracking with fright –

Brian knows. He thinks, I've got to hide this bastard thing. Got to get rid, hasn't he. Won't have the willpower, elsewise. The means to cope with the shrapnel.

Only Brian isn't strong like that. Brian likes to say one thing and do another. Really, he fancies a glance, just to see, just to understand. See what the fuss is about, for one. This thing nobody understands but everybody wants.

And it's funny how ideas set fast:

How it's a fluid movement between intent and the verb.

120

So he's on it now. He pulls the box fully out of the plastic bag. The edges are cold. The locks feel solid. And yet with light pressure, it hisses, and it opens. He raises the lid. He holds his breath.

Inside he can see himself on the bottom.

Brian's face fills the box.

Pandora's box is already tipped out.

11.

Thursday, Diane doesn't come round to spoil Brian's day.

Nobody's asking, but Brian is through here – in the lounge, watching his CCTV monitor, watching his drive, the rain.

Brian's in his chair – the wheelchair in the middle of his world. All days are the same. All days, every hour – trapped. The fat man in his yawning city. Ageing. Smoking and sleeping between damp walls and under bare bulbs. The fat man who sat through power cuts and water shortages. Listened to new riots and masked radicals on his telly. The same chair at the arse-end of Manchester, old capital of the north. The cold city, the blinking city.

Brian: half a man in an old battered chair. Battling to heaven. Finding some new ways to get numb.

Brian dicks about. Brian thinks on making some phone calls. Brian figures he should get hold of Harry, mysterious Harry, and tell him about Noah. But Brian's useless and forgot the tick sheet back in the shop. Lost his marbles; gave up on his pal and took his gear. And he's hating himself, Brian is. Hates how he got so used and fell so far down this rabbit hole. Rubbed up and left to drown. Hates these things he can't understand. Hating the box and so much hindsight. Hating that he's all out of tinnies. Nobody shaking brollies up any walls now.

So he leaves the lounge and makes for the bog. Artex walls to study. Four different walls and a door that won't lock. The downstairs bathroom still wet from his last wash. The tin of exfoliant still green, growing a skin. Sand in the bath; grit in the sink. The skimmer for his skin propped up against the tiles. The light cord a two-metre string. Not clean by your standards; kind of spick and span by his.

But Brian doesn't go in. Brian notices something. Brian stops short of the light cord, swallows hard. Unease is drawn from his toes to his chin. The taste of copper. The dread feeling he's missed something he shouldn't have. The world tipping to its side; sliding around him.

Too late: the hole opens wide and the dread comes through. Fast and hard, hot and dizzy, fear rolling and worse –

The toilet seat is up.

The toilet seat that's never, ever up.

Brian, he breathes *no*. And from behind, muffled, the stairlift starts climbing its chains.

Feedback peals across the house – the tannoy singing its filthy tune. The house is finding its mouth and starting to talk.

The voice says, Will you be my friend, Brian? The voice is modulated; distorted through the tannoy. A sound like slow songs from a cassette player out of juice.

All your doors are locked, the voice says. Really easy when you know how.

Brian's mouth hangs loose.

Come back into the lounge, will you? Let's get a good look at you.

Now it's Brian who's alone with his worst dreams.

Don't play silly buggers, the slow voice says. You listen hard, you'll be right.

I –

The person taps the mic; flat sounds turned to booms on account of the volume.

This on? I meant it. Don't bother with the doors. I'm looking after the bottom of your house.

Brian rolls across the lino, these words washing round him. Brian gets back in the lounge, seated three feet over the debris of his life under bulbs.

Brian hears a noise in the hall. Air moving. Something brushing the floor.

Got your attention, have I? Good.

A louder bang. It's definitely in the hall. Brian strains to look.

There's paper folded up into planes.

Brian is the quiet mouse caught in a trap.

Please let's be friends, the voice says.

A book hits the floor out in the hall.

Brian goes to see.

The Olympic flag bounces softly from the second stair and unfurls.

Brian's archives are coming down the stairs. Planes and books at the bottom of the stairs.

Bananas in pyjamas, says the voice –

Stop it, Brian says. Stop whatever it is you're doing.

There's a rumble over the boards above.

A box of skin splits open, bursting with cream flakes.

Brian recoils from the view in front. He closes his eyes, forward another few feet – so used to the topography of his house he doesn't need to see. That thing they say when you're young: can you get out of your house in smoke, in the dark, in the black. Count the stairs and re-member the steps, our kid. 'Cept you'll have to roly-poly, won't you, our kid –

Brian's in the hall now. He hammers the stairlift buttons but they're all dead.

I told you, the voice says. This is my house now. And I'll save you the trouble of checking the phone, too.

What is this? Brian says. What do you want?

Your skin looks very yellow, Mr Meredith. Are you drinking enough water?

How –

And the state of this place –

Stop it.

Tell me where the box is, and we'll be good pals, you and I.

What box?

What fucking box, Brian? The box you already looked inside.

Brian's chair creaks.

You think we haven't seen everything? That we don't know? You have something you don't need; don't want; don't have any right to have. So make this easy for us both, and you'll have a new friend plus a clean sheet.

Brian shakes his head. Brian's eyes are all wet. Brian's voice is warbling with the stress. I don't know how to help you, says Brian.

Then I'll make it easy. People pay me to make collections. You have something a lot of people want collected.

Right.

The box, Mr Meredith.

How did you get in here, you sneaky bastard?

Cloak-suit. Same way anyone naughty does anything.

And if you take the box, then what?

Like I said. You get a new pal. Friends in right places. People who'll give you all you're after.

You don't know what I want.

Don't I?

And if I don't hand it over?

Well, we all have our insurances. I won't be handling it

myself – you'll meet somebody in town to make the drop. Trams are running today, aren't they. Thursday, isn't it. So you'll take the box into town and meet our contact by memorial column. I've brought a lead container. You'll find this at the bottom of the stairs. The change you'll need for the train is in an envelope on the container.

Who are you?

Could ask the same of you, putting it like that. Had to put your head over parapet, didn't you?

I'm not doing sod all for anyone.

Not what Anubis tells us, is it?

Brian looks at the statue.

Ah. There you are, the voice says.

Upstairs, Brian hears laughing.

Help us, the voice says, and you won't be done for it. We're all friends, Brian. Really great friends.

Through the wall, Brian hears the stairlift chains moving –

Done for it? Done for what?

– The sound his stairlift makes with a full load.

Brian closes his eyes. Emphysemic breathing. Brian reels backwards in the hall, surrounded by his archives and the half-light of outside.

Brian opens his eyes behind his hands. Sees the container on the second step.

Sees the swollen feet coming down from the dark, dark, dark, over the red carpet. Sees her red dress. Sees her red scalp. Sees her red and black skin coming down over the red, red, red carpet.

Everything red.

Diane –

Just in case you thought we weren't serious, the voice says from top of the stairs. The shadow at the top of the stairs.

Ian's voice.

She's better off this way, you know. Better than mud-dying some other shores with that other paki she married. The thought of them breeding –

Brian's chest is crushing him –

So when I've confirmed you've made the drop, an undertaker – pal of mine – pops round, and our matter's resolved. Might even sort your carpets. And for your peace of mind, I've written extra instructions you'll find in an envelope on the top. Bit of cash as we've said. There's some diazepam there too. Help a man of your composition, that. And I'll lock up, of course. Can't have anybody walking in here.

His hand on the wall. His head lolling around.

Diane –

Fail to show up, it's your friends from The Cat Flap next. Talk to anyone, I'll have a lynch mob round here faster than you can spell paedophile.

Diane –

Well go on. Best get moving, hadn't you? Wouldn't want your house growing secrets.

Outside, Noah's Nissan Cherry is parked opposite.

12.

A skinny pigeon follows Brian down the long road town-ways. Mainly it bobbles out in front, but whenever Brian stops to get his puff, which is often, and sometimes for a few minutes at a time, it finds a fence. And when Brian turns off his line to find a lowered kerb, it sits on a post. Sits there and stares at this man in bits.

Brian doesn't feel anything. He's found that new shade of numb. You'd say he had his head up his arse. Pushing himself over the endless cracks and weeds. Caught outside with nothing to live off – just petty cash and the timetable in his pocket. Colin's box in the too-heavy container on his lap. There's a lot of glass, and his wheels crunch on every rotation. Crisp sounds, scuffing sounds. The raised ironworks of these churned roads.

Another corner, and this time Brian sees the pigeon. Brian looks at its feet. Notices how the pigeon's feet are burnt and curled – the feet those silly birds get from standing in their own crap too long.

Shoo, Brian tells it – half convinced he's seeing things. Go on. Get out of it.

The pigeon hops to the floor as Brian stares it down. Staring it out. But he knows these city birds have balls. That they'll make you step over them before they sling their hook. That's why Brian is half minded to squash it.

The pigeon's playing chicken. Playing chicken and winning.

Brian bimbles on, wondering if the traffic lights will still work at the end of the world.

The question being: will he make it by dark.

Brian gets to the tram station and heads up the ramps. At the top, he stops and spits a big white blob. Very dehydrated, now. To have a cold beer, or time in beer gardens. And he wouldn't remember the journey if it weren't for that daft bird.

Through a corridor of smokers, a few Wilbers half-ready to press-gang the vulnerable. Past the kids hanging off the railings. Past the whiteboard and today's delays in red marker. Sweating and counting the floor tiles to keep his mind off death.

Surprise surprise, the ticket man can't see Brian over the plexiglass counter. He almost serves some pushy old wretch instead. The ticket man huffs when he realises, too – that favourite trait of the self-defensive.

Don't get all PC on me, he says to Brian, passing back a penny in change, a card for the train. And he sneers for having to stretch.

Brian says, Thank you. Brian says, See you. Brian over the tiled floor and up gentle inclines.

Brian hits the busy platform, pulls up the blanket and towels his face. The air's close. Heavy weather for heavy times. Pathetic fallacy, your English teachers call that.

The platform, it's a shower of bastards from end to end. It'll be rammed like this all day on account of people and their part-time jobs in town. The closest thing to a commute you'll find. One tram an hour, three days a week, with the newest version of an economy built to match. That's how come it's not worth the walk.

To his right, people in tatty suits buy veg from the

kiosks; trading their Argos tat and their Tesco vouchers for tobacco.

Sometimes, you get people hanging off the trams. Real third-world stuff like that. And even though the Council says they're acting on it, there are bad rumours. Rumours and apathy. Apathy about it all. Of course, the worst rumour, like all rumours, caught hold fast – spreading now and on its way to urban legend. Something about extra voltage through the live wires. A deterrent, they call it.

Brian takes the platform's median and keeps his chin tucked into his chest. His eyes pulled down the barrel of a six-sided cannon. He doesn't want to catch the eyes of others; nobody does. So he opens Ian's envelope. Sees the diazepam and a bleak future beyond. Pulls out a sheet of A4 and the pop-foil pack.

Brian thinks balls to it. Brian bombs the diazepam. Brian hopes for the best – an hour or two of rest.

And Brian starts to read.

The instructions are concise. The paper says:

Bench. Memorial column between four and five. A man will throw money at your feet. You will give your thanks. He will bend down to chat. You will allow him to take the box, which you will have left at your feet. No gimmicks. Nothing else. Try anything on, you'll be destroyed. Remember me with kindness. Ian.

Brian folds the paper and stuffs it back in the envelope. Closes his eyes and thinks of Ian's England –

England and some things he can't unsee. Diane sitting still on the insides of his eyelids –

Somebody on the platform screams.

Jolted, Brian sees a scuffle; people falling over themselves, more screaming and shouting. Hot orange splashed up and across. A man has set fire to a kiosk, and now he's throwing punches at people.

130

God is great! he shouts – plain and flat in a thick Blackburn accent. God is great!

The disenfranchised are making a scene.

Brian boards the train with a ramp and all kinds of fuss. He finds his space and tries to look like he likes a good time. He doesn't do too well.

People are talking about the man on the platform. The usual safe comments about foreigners going home. Don't like our country, don't bleed our country. Goddamn leeches.

These are the normal things you hear.

And whispers on the tram reveal worries about Birmingham. They're coming here, here to Manchester, a woman says. And down there they've gotten into a nuclear plant with bricks and bombs . . . They'll recommission the health trust half-tracks.

And Brian remembers the bulldozers. The smell of burnt stuff.

He remembers the crowds in their masks, the skinheads and their sticks, the policemen and their vans. The radicals at his door. The spit from angry mouths. The lads on buses and trams with chains and bats. Coming paki-bashing? They said. And after weeks – maybe months and more – the soldiers. Soldiers brought home to massacre their own. Six years ago. When war came home and the world went bananas.

Brian remembers this one lad from the telly. He stood against the army with his arms out and his mouth wide. Only a young fella, he was. How, after the bang, he fell to his knees and then backwards, a rock star pose, his heart turned into a bloody rose. And how the shouting grew loud around the cameras, and people took pictures with their phones.

When the city burned from Ancoats to Castlefield, Brian didn't have as good a view. Never did, being half the height of others.

The end of that came with the bullets. The start of this came with harsh words and drafted ships.

Time to become us, or leave us, the Government said.

And more riots and radicals and revolutionaries were made.

Still, Brian doesn't flinch. He's used to these memories. He's reconciled with them. And while he's unfeeling, he definitely isn't deaf. You don't want to be the victim in the crowd.

The tram crosses a bridge over a road. Below, a column of police support vans and half-tracks are filing into the centre.

We were all liberals once, he hears someone else whispering. A young bloke with blonde shagpile hair and a scar running from forehead to chin. And now look at us, he says. Look what fear's done to us all.

13.

Into Manchester Piccadilly. The place they never did bomb. Still shiny in places, too – one of the few refurbishments to last this long.

The concourse, it's not the place to hang around. It's a petri-dish for Wilbers now, and their colonies stand all beady-eyed every few metres. You won't see the captured, of course, because Wilbers do their capturing of people out of sight. But it happens, and everybody knows it. In toilets or taxis. Snatch squads that follow you home. They're always patient, see. Pack-dogs with lengthy stares.

People walk in ruler-straight lines for the exit. Only fools don't bother. You have to keep your eyes down and ignore the taunts. The Wilbers have ways to get your attention – the girls especially. They know the twitches that come with adrenaline. They know when you're glancing, or when you're moving too fast. They know the victims. And they'll pull you up. They'll ask about your day. They'll peel you, expose your cogs, your belts and your gears. They think up places they'll put you to work.

So Brian moves on. Brian keeps a nice face on. The diazepam nowhere near working. Out towards the breeze.

And breathe. Manchester smells of gone-off meat, upturned bins, rotten feet.

A sweeper works the station approach. He's brightly dressed but very small, so while he's hard to miss, nobody pays him any attention. It's windy out here, so half the crap he's trying to bin actually just moves around in circles. He kind of stabs at the floor with his brush, chasing lost papers and crisp packets and dimps. Seems to Brian he's undeterred: there's no way he can let any of it go. And when another bunch of people stamp their fags dead, and go on down the ramp to their jobs, he starts a new circuit. Starts over again. Nothing better to do, no promises round the corner.

I would prefer it, Brian thinks, as he free-wheels downhill towards the sharp edges of town. I would prefer that.

Manchester's like this before dusk. Quiet, or tense, depending on the size of your arms. You expect knives, usually see a scrap, and always feel queasy. Squint, though, and you see the city as it was. Grand old buildings with grand old names. Trees before the neon, and plants before the weeds. It's a safari after dark, course – but . . .

But it's changing, isn't it. It's in a state of flux. Growing wider, eating the suburbs. Bloating hard like a body in a lake. And you talk to this city like mothers talk to naughty sons: I love you, but I don't like you.

On Market Street, a bunch of kids are playing footy against a low-bolted shutter. The ball – bang – is stripped of leather, orange innards poking through a Stanley-knife slit. Bang – the ball off the boarded shopfronts. Kids just having a kickabout on Market Street, ignoring the triple-X on all these signs. White kids, brown kids, black kids besides.

Brian stops a while. Watches their volleys and miss-timed headers. He shouts, Hey! Give an old man a kick!

But the kids ignore him. Everybody does. And twenty yards later, the journey gets boring fast.

Grey fast food and market stalls churning out manky

134

grey produce. Grey walls and wooden panels. Churned up roads and broken bollards –

Outside a pub, a group of squaddies stand with half-pints in a circle, their camo trousers and black t-shirts fading. White faces, brown faces, scabs and scarred knuckles that tell their own stories. Maybe Brits and Afghans who've seen past the politics of older wars. Brown faces, white faces, just big lads goading each other to drink faster, and a load more of it. For friends, they're calling each other some squalid things. Their shoulders still big, but their bellies given over to a welcome lapse in discipline. And Brian has to look down again, thinking of what he and Noah did up in those hills. Who he pretended to be. The lies he told and the fortunes they've sown.

And as he rolls past, the shame stabs harder. Because they somehow mistake him for that person. They clap him solemnly. One of them even salutes.

It's a free country.

He's round towards Deansgate and the ghosts of old bomb attacks. It still feels weird you can't see the Beetham – so long the axle around which this decaying city span. Without the light on, it's a conspicuous absence.

Brian finds a bench and settles next to it. He smiles. Funny how you gravitate to the spaces where the town-planners want you.

Brian checks his baccy tin. Enough for a jay; maybe two thin ones.

And Brian waits for the diazepam cloud. A good little boy doing as he's told.

The memorial column, it's their bright way to say sorry.

It throws a clean wide beam. Keen and clean. From its

base, standing there on Deansgate, by the iron benches and the engraved plaques; the stone wreaths and the fresh flowers, it goes on up for always. Just on and up. Painting cloud, poking stars. That sunset on its side.

But in most ways it doesn't really go with their city. This side of town, the look is red-brick, Victorian, and next to these old mills and arches – the green steel and rust-orange waters of Deansgate Locks – the dish of the light seems too shiny; too obvious. They've set the lamp body and generators into the big oblong of concrete they buried the past with. Steps lead down to the lamp for maintenance, and the circle around it covers at least ten yards. At that size, that circumference, it takes a lot of power to send their thank yous skywards. And that's why it doesn't go. The memorial's a new, enduring thing in a city of entropy.

Every coin has a reverse, though. Stands to reason that from some places – some other views – the memorial glows like another bloody advert for another bloody name. Specially when you can't see how tall it goes. And that's when it makes a perfect fit for this grave new world.

Anniversary or not, survivors or bereaved, tourist – ha! – or traveller, they all come here to look at something. To remember or find a better way to forget.

Brian is half-asleep by his bench. Half-asleep with his box to bear. No energy to scout roofs for snipers, or to wonder how the Beetham, as it fell, missed the railway bridge that runs the outside edge of the memorial site. How it didn't even clip it.

It's dark and growing darker, and the column puts everything into deep contrast, it's so bright. The red viaduct's a muddy brown. The concrete's turned a slick black. It's imprinted when you blink, throws shutters across your vision when you turn away.

He sees the night in, sitting there. Sees low clouds lit up and speared by the beam. Hears the city coming to life around him – the homeguard soldiers getting out and about, and after so much fanny. Their own war at home.

He hears sirens. A procession of police spreading themselves into a net.

In silhouette, a figure comes towards Brian. He can't be sure if it's aiming his way. Jealously, he grips the box and prepares for the moment he must let go. He feels disconnected; dreamy.

Closer, he sees it's too small to be anyone he knows. Some kid – probably working pockets like every other opportunist under these stars. Until he hears a little voice.

Hello Mr Brian, she says. A little girl, seven or eight, no more. She's sitting on the bench now, swinging her legs. She's in dungarees and jelly sandals. Nineties clothes; the type of clothes kids wear without a worry.

She smiles at him, missing teeth and all.

You're Brian, she says.

Brian doesn't react. Maybe the diazepam, maybe something else. But he's seen her before –

My mummy says you're sad.

The little girl from Inner Sole.

Brian's tummy starts to turn. He feels the temperature in his cheeks. He doesn't want to be seen alone with a young girl. The way people think in this day and age –

You're not on your own, are you? he whispers.

The little girl shakes her head.

Mummy says you're special.

The bad feeling pulled across in two black curtains. The bad, bad feeling –

Does she now?

Constance nods tersely.

Yep. That you're a fish out of water, she says. You want to walk, she said –

Now come on, little one –

Mummy says you have to come.

Come where? What's your name?

The little girl stands up and curtseys.

I'm Constance, she says.

That's an unusual name, says Brian. Let's find your mam shall we?

Constance shakes her head from her hips upwards. Swaying left and right.

No.

No?

No.

Well, we'll have to call the council, won't we? And they'll come and take you and put you in a home.

Constance laughs. Constance runs circuits round the bench. Constance says, You're mean, Mr Brian. Pleee-ee-ase come. Mummy wants to help you. My daddy wanted to help but you didn't listen to him. And when you come we can play Top Trumps and Playstation and Tiddly-Winks –

Brian chokes as he tries to swallow. Brian looks round for a call box.

I'll ask you one more time, Brian says. I'll count to three.

But Constance has started to cry. Dark clouds are rolling over the sunshine. Her wet face lit up wet and white by the column.

Now don't make a scene. Just tell me where your mam is.

A figure flickers on the bench besides Constance. A person in strobe – flickering on and off. Sitting perfectly still on the bench, looking right at Brian.

138

Mummy's here, the figure says.

All at once: the girl who knocked on for money; the girl from Inner Sole –

Gone again.

Constance grins and cuddles up to thin air. And before Brian's eyes, thin air pulls Constance closer.

Brian forgets to breathe. *You.*

Put it down and we'll get you out of this.

Who are you?

I'm Juliet. Don't look so frightened – the suit's just protection. If they see me, they'll kill us both.

The edges are fuzzy. The buildings are tilting. Brian goes, Did you –

Brian, it's no cliché to say there isn't time. Ian's contact will be here in forty-three seconds. You will be dead in forty-six. You're going to have to listen.

Brian's stomach on a lift platform north. The blanket around him letting in the cold. The wool getting heavier.

You can't see it, Juliet tells him, and nor can the shooter on the viaduct, but there's a vehicle in front of you. Cloaked the same way you know, just bigger. On three, we'll push you on board. It's a van; more than big enough.

Tick.

The buildings tilting further, the earth spinning faster. Nothing ever simple.

Tock.

And no, you don't have much choice, I'm afraid.

Bloody right I don't, says Brian. Not when you put it like that.

It's this or you're the proud owner of three new holes. Constance?

Yes?

Off you go.

The girl takes four steps and disappears. Brian can't wrap his head round it.

No time like the present, this woman called Juliet says, behind him now.

And Brian moves, moves, moves.

As the first shot comes.

As the second hits something loud; sends a bouquet of sparks through the black.

As he moves through a pane of Manchester and into a tin.

14.

Juliet doesn't say much – she's all white knuckles and hard lines. She looks in her mirrors and stands on the gas. Constance is in her child seat, kicking her legs.

They belt off down Chester Road from the memorial site. She parks the van near Old Trafford football stadium. The theatre of shattered dreams, skeletal, shelled out, derelict like the rest. A perfect case study from a ruined city. The wasteland and scrub outside it; a surprising amount of crap built up in so little time. Those opposite poles, money and the monastic, smashed together.

Brian, Brian has had it up to here. Brian is shouting and banging about. But Brian can't do much from his position and never truly can – an impotence he resents more than the circumstances. He's having a bad trip. A right old ding-dong. He's claustrophobic and won't have any of it. Who the hell is this bitch? These kind of thoughts. The thoughts you assume nobody will ever hear. The thoughts you're told to keep to yourself.

Juliet comes into the back. She isn't wearing much, a shabby crop top and running shorts. The marks of a big pregnancy on a slim frame are clear. Her hard face. She pulls a shawl round her shoulders and sits back against the panel opposite him. Not a shred of make-up now. Not a shred of self-consciousness. Her cheeks sallow perhaps because she doesn't make the time to eat properly. The van austere in the same way. High-

141

top Transit; tortoiseshell MDF to finish. Older than Constance's jellies, even.

Going to quit being a drip?

Brian spits on the floor.

Calm down and listen to me. You're safe in here.

I've lost my home –

You'd lose more than that hanging about on that plaza.

Ian promised me.

Ah, Ian. Promised you legs, didn't he? All that war-tech they spoke about. Well, not before he tattooed a Hitler-tache on your top lip, son.

He promised. The box for his word.

Promises aren't hard to break.

You have to trust people. It's all we have left –

Juliet snorts.

You know in your guts that's bullshit. They promised my husband, too – and you saw what the bastards did to him.

Brian looks down. Brian's hairs tingle.

The realisation and the revelation.

Tight guts and hard frowns. The man in the corner; the man on stage.

Could've guessed by the van, Brian says. A resignation to his voice. And the charity work, he goes, the shoe-shop – you and him for all this time?

Juliet shrugs.

You were meant to notice, yes, she says. It's everybody else you have to fool.

Why me?

It's a kind of fate that's brought this box here, has it not?

Don't talk daft.

No more daft than what they killed my Colin over. The ideas you heard at that conference for little boys in big suits. Nationalism bores the piss out of me, love – but the men in that place wanted so much more. Left unchecked, Ian's going to become a very big problem for your country.

Don't want no bloody riddles neither, Brian tells her. I just want my home back.

Juliet nods. Brian swears he catches a half-smile.

But it's not just you, Juliet says. Not like you're important, is it? We've tabbed your friend Noah for ages, too. Mixes with the wrong type, doesn't he, your man? And I'll tell you this for bloody free: he's playing the game, he is. Working for everyone. This thing my Colin had was not for stealing. This thing you'll leave with me.

Brian asks what she means about Noah. Not knowing if she knows Noah has gone.

And Brian would have a lot more questions if he weren't so sick or tired, sick and tired.

Well, you were second fiddle, Juliet says. We knew you had contact with him. That's why you were interesting for a time. But him – Noah. For starters, you realise there's probably no Garland? No Garland, no pay-out, no rewards. There might've been – a client of his sometime ago maybe. But from all we can gather, he's quite dead now. Seems your Noah gets his info about their meetings the same place we do, and thought he'd look at our box himself. Wanted new ideas for himself, I expect. Or more likely, he's batting for his council chums again.

Brian doesn't want to say anything more about Noah. The names in his office screamed of a man whose loyalty you have to buy. Brian, he's usually taken for a mug, but he's not completely stupid.

And the spies always find their eyes.

Besides, there's a different question on his tongue:

Who are they?

143

Juliet's mouth curls at one corner. They.

Do you believe in God, Brian?

Doesn't answer my question, that.

But do you?

Selling God after all, are you? he says. What's that got to do with anything?

I wondered.

I don't bloody know, do I?

I think you barely believe in yourself, Juliet says. Your unreal life in this unreal place.

How do you know so much about me? asks Brian.

Juliet looks down. Seen one you've seen them all. I've met a hundred yous across a hundred worlds trying to find the right one.

Bollocks you have.

Have to do your research when something like this crops up. I'm not asking you to believe me.

Aye, and I'm not asking you to tell whopping lies.

Course, you don't need to believe in something if it happens anyway. There's a big gap between faith and proof – a difference you obviously can't be arsed with. And since I don't have time to faff around, I'm happy to let you think what you like. You want your house back, you leave it to us. You want your life back, you leave it to me. Just don't ask bloody questions when you say you don't have time for answers. Let's just say I work for people beyond these walls. And that the world doesn't revolve around you.

Seems all of you work for somebody, Brian says. But you know he's gone, don't you? Noah?

Juliet nods.

The box. Can't explain the bleedin' mess –

I know, Juliet says. Which is why I want it back.

What did it do to him?

144

Does different things to everybody. It's a dangerous thing.

Convenient, that, Brian says.

Hardly, says Juliet. I've spent long enough trying to find it. Curiosity and cats, Brian. Just for Christ's sakes tell me you didn't open it too.

Juliet scans Brian with some kind of rod. He's shaking, our Brian. From the cold and the adrenaline. The endless comedown.

He opened it all right. And it opened him –

What has the box done?

They're in the van, the surfaces turning damp with the cold. Juliet runs the rod lengthways from top to tail. It bleeps a lot. She keeps huffing, put out. She's really cheesed off with him. She tells Brian he's like all the men she's ever known.

It was empty, Brian tells her. Empty. I could see my face in the bottom of it. That's what I don't get.

You can't see air, she says back, concentrating. But you damn well know it's there.

Am I going to die?

We're all going to die.

You know what I meant. Like Noah. He melted. He bubbled up and melted.

Juliet smiles coldly. She clips her voice. I already told you. I don't know. From what we've seen, different things seem to happen to different people. And that's because it's not meant to be looked at, opened, used. It's part of something else. It's a component of a project you lot never deserved to know about.

Diane's dead, says Brian. In my house, on my stairs. I have nothing to give anyone.

I know.

Dead over your box, though. That's why you tell me what's in it and what the bloody hell I do now.

Colin already said. My lad you all robbed from.

I don't remember.

He told you on that stage. He came to make offers, and nobody wanted it on his terms. Or everybody did –

I don't remember.

You take too many drugs is why. You're all the same.

If you mean we all have a vice.

She looks down at his tail, still waving this strange wand across the flesh. The van is perfectly quiet but for the hum of the rod's battery. Perfectly dark but for the weak strip along the roof.

Juliet puts a hand on Brian's bulbous knee. Why do you pretend you're not all there, Brian? Is it easier?

You're at it again. I don't know what you mean.

Your mother made you believe something.

Mam's dead.

You still dream of her.

I –

Juliet pokes his thigh.

Your tail – do you call it that? And the way you eat your hair because you think it makes you invulnerable. Because you read that in some old Japanese books. Because it's a nicer way round what you really are.

And what am I?

You scrub your skin because you see scales. You skim the water. You live your mother's words because you're frightened of your own. A life under the gaze of her watchtower.

She's dead, Brian says again. He's dizzy suddenly.

She's dead, and you're not. But you should have died, shouldn't you? Don't usually last so long, people with your condition. That's special enough, isn't it – that you didn't?

146

Dizzy and sick –

They said it was a miracle. That I was –

Juliet smiles again. We say miracles breathe through gaps in knowledge.

Sick and dizzy –

I've seen it all, she tells him. I told you. You were lucky enough to get an arsehole, a bladder. Most with your condition get nothing at all; die before they're nine or ten.

I'm special, Brian tells her. Now he's starting to weep.

But only because you survived. And all that in spite of your mother. More through luck than care. Because your mother wouldn't allow the surgery; wouldn't accept what she'd birthed.

Stop it, Brian says.

Religion dictates the funniest things, Juliet says. Though it worked out for you. A miracle's made on the back of your luck.

Please –

Your mother couldn't face the deformity, so she made you believe the myth. She didn't believe in doctors, did she? You and her in the hospital she didn't want to visit. Other people's blood; other people's bodies. Because yours is your own and should never be sullied. And she took you to the Olympics and then she went and died on you.

Brian wretches. Brian has wretched so many times before –

You poor, poor man, Juliet says.

Juliet dries Brian's face. She passes him bottled water and invites him to take sips. The bottle is cold and slippery. Constance is sleeping in the front seat, bundled into a fleece blanket.

Juliet asks how long since he last got high. Brian tells her the truth. Juliet shakes her head.

Juliet tells Brian some stories. She's fierce about Colin. She tells him in clichés and hollow proverbs, just so he can understand. She says bland things like: We've all lost something precious. It's how you deal with it that matters.

Brian sniffs. Brian's putting a brave face on.

Brian's terrified of Juliet.

Of what she knows.

They're still by Old Trafford, parked between the divots of heavy tracked vehicles. The early hours of some day or the other.

I didn't choose to come to your version of Manchester, Juliet says.

You said you weren't going to tell me why you're here.

It's just a way of speaking, says Juliet. But you know you're in trouble. The people who took my fella aren't the forgetful type. They want what you brought here.

Why?

You care now?

I don't care about anything.

Terrified.

Good, says Juliet. Because when they catch up with you, they will take everything.

15.

They drive on. Silent. Under lamps and strobe-flash neon.

Juliet parks in shadows and covers the Transit in camo netting. She's gone four minutes at most; obviously well practised on the weighty matters.

Juliet has itchy arms after that. She opens the van's side door. The netting falls about her as a dress.

Best kip here, hadn't you, she goes to Brian. She scratches herself with bitten nails. We'll move first light – think on the fly. I know some people over in Matlock; you could stay there till we've sorted Ian.

Sort my own mess, can't I, says Brian – stoic again, or just stubborn.

Juliet laughs. She slaps the van's hull. Skirts the issue.

Can't use the cloak tonight, I'm afraid. Old girl'd have nowt left in her by morning.

Brian doesn't say anything else. Brian can see her nipples through the top, but unlike that first time, she's turned asexual and sinew-y. A witch. Her dimples have turned to lines. A sorceress. She has been hollowed out – a tough, pretty thing turned soft inside. A wretch.

Brian looks behind her. He doesn't know where they got to. The way you see places differently at night.

But he knows where the box is. And something in him wants the box back. Wants the box to keep. Because it's the only thing to his name; a new currency now trust has gone. An asset that makes him relevant.

Asexual Juliet has a peaceful face owing to sleep. Brian had meant to put diazepam in her flask, but fell asleep himself before he got chance. Constance is still sleeping in her fleece blanket. Little Constance with the big gob.

Brian wishes he'd asked Juliet what her game is.

Brian makes his move and grabs the box. His box – the one he collected for himself on the floor of Noah's bunker.

Over to the doors; the outside beyond. He's not waiting to find out.

Not waiting around to find out about Matlock or otherwise – the week has taught him that. Sure, best laid plans don't come to pass, but he isn't staying in a tin cage and having someone else decide for him. You want to win, you go in with your studs showing.

His chair creaks as he cracks the door; his eyes closed like that helps. The net's a big problem but mechanical noises by night are bigger.

Still: better out on his shattered land than trapped in here with a witch.

Brian makes his move. Brian slides out the access ramp, inch by inch, squeal by squeal.

And Constance hears him.

She peers through the slat below the headrest, rubbing her eyes.

Where are you going, Mr Brian?

For a damn tinkle, kid.

Mummy says you're not allowed.

Your mam's asleep. She can't tell grown-ups what to do.

We are not in your city any more, the little girl tells him. We've moved house.

But Brian is gone and rolling away – faster than you've ever seen him move.

All signs say Salford Quays. Stands to reason when you think of the roads away from the memorial light.

From the tilt of the Earth towards the moon, Brian knows he's outside, alone, in curfew hours. Alone without a watch and rolling towards the bright city lights with the box rattling over his mess of a knee. The memorial light as tall as the clouds.

Soon, the sky breaks and soaks the land. Brian's wheels start to pull a fine spray from the tarmac. Fast hands banging the wheels as though he's rowing; fast hands that slip too often and twist him sideways in jerks.

Flat Salford Quays with the tramps by the waterfront. Flat Salford Quays with pretty lights and lock-tighter doors – the BBC folk in compounds like forts. And the van, it's well behind him now he's taken two corners. Constance could raise all the hell she wanted – he'll have a better chance of hiding.

Brian stops for breath. Swearing at the weight of the box. Alone in the company of racing thoughts – the thoughts of a man out of options.

A man off by the waterfront has his hood pulled tight. He's looking out over the water, a thick rope running from the railings into the dark.

Water taxis.

Brian forgot about the water taxis.

In fairness to Brian, pretty much everyone does. Few years back, they built an extra canal – the first in a hundred years – and another venture they were excited about before the riots. It runs from the Quays out towards the

Trafford Centre. Then, it was a golden chance to roll between the Quays and the shops. A novelty, but a profitable one.

Now, the canal's a nasty strip of water between two derelict holes.

They were brighter days, those. The BBC coming north and the Quays finally filling its rooms. The gondolas, very English gondolas, lazing across the waterfront. Lazy execs and writers getting stoned on their dinner breaks.

Novel businesses died during and after the riots. This one drowned.

New business came. Bad men with bad hearts. Same as any route you can move along, they run coke and the rest up these dark channels.

And Brian remembers these water taxis.

Brian has a lot of thoughts at once.

Like the first ant, you look closer to see more. Surely enough, a dozen men appear. Cresting the water edge, their heads bobbing up and down; in and out of view.

For all the static between his ears; the fuzz and the fretting, Brian knows it might be the best way to skip town. Nobody would look for anybody on these waters at this time. The worst place the council could send their bootboys.

The canals. A perfect place for an inland mermaid.

I have nothing to give you, Brian tells the man by the water. I just need to get out of here.

Nie rozumiem, the man says. He's a heavy-set Pole. His mouth is a scar running cheek to cheek.

Brian points desperately at the boat and into the black. Please, he says.

Nie rozumiem, the Pole says, shrugging.

Brian doesn't move. Doesn't know what he's being told.

The Pole rubs his forefinger and thumb together. Cash only, Brian guesses. You earn trust and service by paying up front – and by paying plenty.

Brian looks dumbstruck. But I don't have any cash, he says. I just need to get away from here.

The Pole raises his arms.

Pierdol sie! he goes.

What? Look –

The Pole flaps his hands away from him. The international language of shoo. *Spadaj*! *Ostrzegam Cię*!

Brian gets it at last. Unwanted and weeded out. Those best laid plans all gone to muck.

Debil! The Pole shouts from the railings.

The other men, smoking by their own boats, turn to see. Their view makes Brian little more than a floating head.

Brian roams. Smokes and roams. The water in the night. The clouds and the lights.

The rain stops. The Imperial War Museum with a shiny roof – a great sleeping beetle.

Brian, he knows they'll be looking for him soon. The girls, Constance and Juliet, giggling and ganging up –

Thinking, Dogs with barks need muzzles.

Thinking, Next time.

By a footbridge, he finds a pile of wet cardboard. It's sodden and drooping at the corners. Someone's last bed, perhaps, though not tonight.

Brian remembers what Noah said once. They were up on Werneth Low. He talked about how the best survivalists stashed baccy, alcohol, printed encyclopaedias for doomsday. Stuff to sell, stuff to drink, knowledge for the days beyond the internet – or worse, to brighten the new dark age.

Those days came. Those days are now. And all Brian stashed was a blanket and a last corner of sniff.

Brian takes the time to wrap up tight; the old blanket a loyal friend – as loyal as the unease and the dread.

Struggling to space the cardboard. Struggling to make his bed at God knows what the time is.

There are things he can't handle from the chair – gravel, grass, steps – but he's determined he'll get this one thing right.

Soon, he unfolds himself and leaves his chair; puts weight through his wrists and rolls to his side. Shoulders the hard ground. On his back, he pulls soggy cardboard around him as best he can. Like a sausage roll, the more you look at him.

On his back, vulnerable and wheezing, those black curtains drawing close, he gets the idea that everything you dread never usually comes to pass.

But still he dreads more rain. More rain and worse.

The wrong kind of water –

Day dreaming at night of warm sun and morning light and salt over his skin. Everything's all right in the day time. Everything's all right in the day time. Everything's all right in the day time –

But he knows what good his dirty little habit does; the knowledge he has. He rolls up his sleeves. He looks over his forearms. He smiles. He has something. And he nibbles hairs from the wrists – the longer hairs; the finest hairs. And he swallows, hard to do when you're flat-out, and he chokes on the hairs, the fine little hairs. And he pulls the cardboard to his mouth and sucks hard – the taste and the wet –

Our Brian, our half-man on the roll, our man Brian hiding and still –

Our Brian, wrapping cold fingers round the box like it's all he has left.

Falls –

Into –

Sleep.

Into nightmares. Broken sleep for broken men on their backs on the half-shores of Salford.

Apples, worms; cables, cars. Post-it poems. The car by the lamp post.

The watchtower in the sharpline nest.

The sea, then. The wet sand. The watchtower as the lighthouse now.

Somebody close – the breath in his hair.

Sitting on a knee, a knee by the sea.

You've ruined everything. My little –

Mam.

For Brian, it never ends.

Three facts:

He wakes on Salford's half-shore to a searing pain in his back.

It's raining – it's always raining –

He lies in a circle of pigeons.

A circle of goddamn pigeons looking over him, strutting around him.

The pain in his back knocks him sick –

A hand wrapped round and clamping does nothing. Just wet, wet heavy cotton and bits of grit.

The box still there, the box in his other hand, his back screaming.

Early hours Saturday. The blue-grey hours before alarms and paper rounds.

His hand clasped, squeezing, pushing.

You didn't need clairvoyance to see the rain coming. Long thin drops going straight down – cutting margins into the world. Saturday's pigeons not arsed, the pigeons just waiting.

Piss off, Brian goes. Go on. Out of it, you little gits.

The pigeons are never arsed. Ballsy types, these. Waiting forever, they are.

So Brian swipes, shrieks, the cardboard tearing along the wettest seams. He looks down. And then.

And then.

And then there's a pigeon on him – two more and then three – three altogether, all pecking, and more coming.

Brian screams, brushes them off. Screams and fights the birds from his tail.

The birds peck and tear at his blanket. They go at his pale skin and at his scales. The blood starts to well in little centimetre pits; the blood running in stripes across the whitest, whitest skin.

Oh God, Brian says.

Nobody around. Nobody around. Too early.

He screams. Awake for sure, now. He screams and crawls, an impression of a smashed crab; a broken tripod, his hands cut over harsh ground. Dragging Colin's box, which scrapes and bobbles and catches on its edges –

The other pigeons come round, come about. A half-circle, all closing on his tail and his meat and his body. His chair's beyond them – his only way out with any dignity, but maybe not fast enough. And screaming like he is, the girls will find him faster.

The water laps the concrete behind him, so he aims himself that way and keeps hoping, his eyes fixed hard on the birds by his feet, all of them taking pot-shots basically.

The edge, and the railing. He pulls his body into a seated position, with his tail sticking out towards the birds, his back to the water and all those bad ideas.

The box in his hand. His chair beyond the birds. The birds at his toes.

Brian leans forward, shouts, Fuck you, and reaches into his top pocket as the first bird strikes his webbed toes.

Brian takes out that last corner of sniff. A finger in, a finger out, a finger in his nose.

Enough to take off the sting. Enough to tighten his grip.

Just water left, now. And the birds take chunks off his shins. The birds screaming with war, their beaks shining with the red and the wet, his blanket torn a little more.

Bad luck dumps Brian into water that's even colder than it looks. Black below and blue above, and turning over himself so he doesn't know which way's which. The gasp on impact, his chest compressed by the chill of it.

Brian's eyes are on their ends, his ears full, his heart smashing out. In the water and churning over – clothes round him heavy, the chair and blanket gone now, the box heavy but still in one hand, pulling him between this life and another. The wrong water, the lights across the water every time he surfaces, the pigeons on the concrete laughing.

Brian doesn't have long. Brian waves like it matters. Like he means something. His meat is tense and writhing under him. He's taking gobfuls of water that he swallows and chokes on.

But God or good fortune listens. Brian feels hands under his pits, in his pits. An outboard motor he hears churning the black; the loud wind a torment over wet skin. *Keep hold of the box –*

157

A hard line crosses his back as he rises free; a hard line smashed across every notch of his spine – a bar across his seared back, screaming. He is scraped out of Quays by a man in a boat. The box in the bottom. His body collapses then. He is racked over the ribs of the hull.

Lucky, the man says.

The Pole says.

The Pole throws tarpaulin over his catch.

I am Jan, he says. He says it *yan*. You must become warm, Englishman.

Brian holds up a hand he can't feel, winces vaguely as it flops back to his belly. He nods. He closes his eyes to a purple starfield. Feels the shivers that rattle the boat.

In and out of it. Eyes open and closed. His back throbbing, his hands and toes sparkling with pins and needles.

Jan cuts the outboard. It purrs as the boat stops. We paddle, he says.

Brian thinks of a tune. Hums the tune. *Row, row, row the boat, gently into hell –*

And they skim along the waterway, the pair of them. Brian can barely see for the pain, but Jan has a head torch he turns on for a second, every twenty seconds or so. It's to make sure he's on course – about all he can do to minimise the risk of tramps on the banks taking their shots or worse. The bushes and the naked branches jump out in the white. The oily water shines and birds take flight.

On the water, it's black and gets blacker, as though the boat is travelling across a thin film of glass up in outer space. With the outboard off, only Jan's paddles make a delicate noise, the rowlocks creaking, and more often than that, silent. The sky lightening for another dawn.

Life is but a dream –

A dream you leave and slip back into – a dream cut

158

through with the harsh light from Jan's head torch.

The light on. The light off. Breathe. The light on. The light off. Breathe. The light on. The light off. Breathe. The light on –

This time, Jan swears – something blunt in Polish. He doesn't waste a moment – hammers the light off, dives down alongside Brian, pulling the excess tarp over his body. He stays there – the pair of them lying parallel, peas in a pod, with their legs out under the rowing bench. The rowlocks judder and ring.

Brian is in a lot of pain, murmuring to himself, humming his rowing boat song.

Jan tells him to button it. He says, You must become silent. Towpath.

Brian didn't know what he means. You wouldn't, a pain like the one in his back.

Silent or I brain you, Jan says.

His face is close now. He's serious. He really means it.

Hands to his sides, Brian tries his hardest.

Good, Jan says, still whispering. Good.

And they drift, the pair of them. Both lying there on the wet wood, running through the veins of Manchester.

Jan's torch picks out the distance in longer intervals now. Can never be too cautious; the unknown dangers on these canal paths getting dodgier the farther along they travel.

It's light enough to see, now, nudging five AM or roundabouts, but the details are given to shifting. A man becomes a tree; a bush becomes a Wilber tent. The kind of tricks your brain plays when adrenaline takes over.

Next time round, Jan flashes his torch over Brian. He gets himself a decent look at the man shivering below him in the hull.

159

Where are you from, fish man?

Brian struggles to say, exhaling hard to get the words out. His back is screaming. He needs more rest. The wool is heavy with water.

You want medicine?

Brian nods pathetically.

What've you got?

Jan pulls a hip flask from his padded jacket.

A lot of times this work. Do not smell first.

Brian takes the hip flask and makes a big deal out of opening it.

Go, says Jan.

Brian takes a slug. It chokes him, and it burns him, and it's everything apart from nice.

Burn hole in mountains! Jan says, chuckling. He takes the flask back.

Brian coughs and splutters.

The hell's that filthy stuff? he says, his eyes streaming.

Moonshine, you call.

Run bloody cars on that –

You feel better, yes.

Worse, you lunatic bastard.

You like.

I don't like anything.

You like it. And now you tell me where you from.

Brian tells him.

And where does fish man go.

To hide.

Jan chuckles some more.

We all run from something.

Brian's grip tightens round the box handle. He sees Diane for a second – Diane in the ribs of the boat; her swollen feet; the whine of the stairlift motor –

What is this box, fish man? Nearly take you to bottom.

160

It's – it's empty.

Why do you keep?

Sentimental value, Brian tells him. Listen, you got a got a fag I can ponce?

Mm?

A cigarette.

Nie.

You have to help me find somewhere.

You will be safe with me. We find you chair. I know men from the hospital. My wife –

I need a phone, Brian says.

Phone, yes. We try –

You don't understand. They will kill me. I have nothing –

No, no. Nobody kill you. You can trust me of this.

Brian trusts Jan till about when the grappling hook comes over the bush line. By hook or by luck, it catches the nose of the boat, rolling them slightly, the hull smacking the water top like an open palm over wood. The wrong place at the wrong time, they'd say in the old news – till every street was the wrong place, that was.

Next news this filthy man comes out from the scrub – the kind of man you call wild-eyed – with a crossbow at forty-five degrees and the rope's end looped round his ankle. He's calling some friends to see.

Oi! Little and large out 'ere, he's shouting, his little white eyes open wide, kicking his foot.

Jan stays very still and leans back on the rowing bench.

Brian, he's paralysed. Muffling himself on account of the fright.

What you doing on here this time of day? the man on the towpath says. What's your game, white-boy? Can't be doing no fishing down here.

161

I am lost, Jan says. I want go south.

I bet. What's this dirty accent? Polish?

I am taking injured man for help.

English, cunt, or you're having it.

I am take this man home.

The man on the towpath points down the waterway.

Wouldn't sail down there. Bare Wilbers on marches. Lost two lads down that way only yesterday. Heads on poles. Bad news, bad times.

Two new faces bob out behind the shabby man.

Turns out it's the big cue for Polish Jan.

Jan throws himself backwards and hammers the outboard off its tilt, a fluid motion that betrays practise making perfect – the only way anybody pulls order out of trauma. And by now he's throttled in and yanking the engine cord out and over his stomach. Just like that. The engine starts, he kicks the hook free, and they're away.

Do widzenia –

Two bolts miss.

Jan guns the boat up the waters between Salford and Castlefield. On past the ghosts of old manufacturing, industries rusting in the north's harrowing rain, the scrapyards taken back by weeds. Sure enough, there's a Wilber camp in one clearing, barricaded on three sides by tipped lorries, and a group in there round a bonfire, laughing. The smoke smells rotten – smells wrong. But there aren't patrols, despite the warnings, and the early sun sluicing through the tall, tall buildings somehow catches them in better moods.

Brian catches himself halfway to praying. *You know what, God –*

Ahead, their cityscape crests into view – a throat of concrete arches to pass under before you're in the belly of it.

I were dreaming, weren't I? And it never felt like this –

Jan turns off the motor and taps Brian around.

Psst. Psst. Do you hurt, fish man? On your behind? Do not worry much. My wife helps.

My back, yes, Brian tells him, reaching round, his leg wounds long since clotted. Something bad's going off. I don't . . . how far can you take this boat?

Excuse? I do not understand.

I mean – I mean if I pay you. If I can pay you, somehow, how far will you take me?

Oh. Our engine small, friend. But with more fuel, Bury, to maybe Rochdale. Through city and many miles past. How long do you want to run?

Forever, Brian tells him.

There are tunnels under city, Jan tells him. Lot of men hide there.

Not without big bloody guns they don't, Brian says. Low enough as we are, pal. Water rats here, aren't we. Six feet bloody under as we are. Why'd you want to go lower? With all them whores and pushers?

Jan scratches his cheek. His stubble.

Sorry, he says. The police?

Brian shakes his head. It's the hopelessness of everything cutting harder. The sheer bloody scale of everything.

Just need a phone, Brian says. I have a man –

Around them, the water has turned to rainbow. The sun's coming out with his hat on. The oil lit from the side; the low light chopping shadows from the walls.

Just can't be doing with the wait, Brian says.

Jan looks ahead, down at Brian. Pathetic Brian wrapped in tarp.

Their rainy city is a grey area in more ways than one. The extra bit of cash, the extra lack of dignity, means the

163

person you'd call decent in the old days you might call a bad egg now. And yet without trust or time, people tell their stories easy. They take a few to justify new jobs in the world gone bad. Fast words make quick bonds.

We're all thieves and beggars now.

Jan has his sob-story. It plays well as they row through the centre of the planet's first industrial city. As they hear the shouts and the bird-cries of an early morning in the old man's land of cotton smog and deaf workers.

I was farmer in Kent before problems, Jan says. I collect vegetables. They poisoned crop and took one of my childs through tunnel in Channel. I work here as taxi-man for two years. Now I don't have job, but I speak your English.

You get on pretty well, Brian says. You get on just right.

I learn English from your newspapers. I am resourceful. My wife cleans clothes in Didsbury. I am working for a man in the city. It is not as bad.

Friends in the city. Only way anybody gets on, Brian says. So you . . . so you sail down here with gear?

Jan shakes his head. Banana. Eggs. Meat.

Brian laughs.

The city rolls around them. Like an old film – the city on a reel.

And Jan's sob-story plays on as Brian sees the first marcher. The first marcher on a foot bridge, and his big dirty flag – the marcher peering over the railings that cage the canal. Brian on his back, hands on his belly, just looking up at this handsome kid. A joint on his lips; a bunch of big empty words over his shoulder.

And behind them, Brian sees more of the early-morning marchers and their shiny new flags and painted banners, still wet. And realises –

Birmingham got here by morning.

164

They pull close to the stonework of a canal bridge. The reflected arches make a pair of wobbling circles in the oily water. Brian sees impossible graffiti in the curve above. Thinks about the protestor and his joint; thoughts plunging him into years they thought they'd done with. The rhetoric and the retching.

We stop here, says Jan. Can you sit, fish man?

Brian tries. No. Jan. It's all going to kick off –

Jan pulls out his hip flask.

I know. I hear radio. But try to sit! Or you want more of this?

Brian tries. Brian's back sears in spider-lines from his arse to his neck. He winces, blinks the purple edges away. He steadies himself and looks down the river. All washed up.

Back the other way, the view makes his mouth fall wide. The spiked clock tower of Manchester cathedral peers down over railings and roadway fences – its face leaning forward as if to judge.

Brian lurches round, the panic in his voice.

What road is this?

Jan points up.

This? Victoria Bridge. You see cathedral. It is beautiful place. Is a safe place, here, fish man. Do not worry.

Brian hisses.

Why have we stopped?

Do not worry! Jan says.

At the water's edge, there's a plank of rotten timber maybe half a foot wide. Jan ties the boat off on a rusty-red pole. He caps the knot with a rubber washer.

Jan catches Brian's baffled look. He says, No step here. We make a tunnel.

It strikes Brian as a lot of work. An odd thing to find, to plan. A joke –

165

But you cannot see from road on our head, Jan says. He points at the bushes. These tree is camouflage.

Jan hops on to the timber – the narrowest jetty you'll ever see. He starts pulling stones from the bridge, and lays them two by two on their sides. Soon, in just minutes, Brian is gawping into a black hole. Jan passes him a Maglite; an old weighty thing – a reassurance. He motions to shine the torch down the hole. Brian does. Brian makes out the rubble of hasty digging. Then, something glints outways – a light moving across their faces and in their eyes.

A mirror –

Good, says Jan, beaming, the cat with all the cream. Wilbers have not found my family.

And big strong Jan carries our Brian inside.

Big strong Jan carries Brian in backwards.

Mud and mortar turns to concrete slabs – dripping, damp owing to the cold. There's a spare dinghy, scuffed on account of how they have to drag it through the hole.

The funnel opens out.

Jan lays Brian out on a mattress in the dull. These are boiled clean sheets – meticulously, surprisingly clean sheets. Brian catches himself staring into the cotton weave. A spider runs over the corner.

He turns over and props up his head. Big strong Jan has made a nest.

The nest, it's a corner of an underground car park, sectioned off by cars on their sides, the cars criss-crossed with rope for wet clothes, the wet clothes dripping on to reclaimed carpets, rugs, offcuts of underlay. Heavy fabrics swing from shop-style racks, and Jan's put boards up, too – cork and MDF and that useless two-ply stuff

166

you find in forgotten skips. Strikes Brian as a project, doesn't it. The kind of room you add to, pile on top of. Hide things in. It looks like a carboot sale. All soft lines and busy space.

Jan's family sits across the way – across a dozen mismatched rugs at odds through pattern. Two kids in duffel coats with hoods up. A young but withdrawn woman between them. They're huddled round something Brian can't see.

Jan's hip-flask bounces to Brian's side without a word.

More, says Jan. Take. Jan points at himself. How you say it. How you say. Puts eyes on chest.

Brian slowly unscrews the cap.

Jan turns and speaks to his family. He doesn't say anything Brian can understand, but his arms are flying about.

The family turn together, looking down, coming closer. Brian, he gets the trepidation, but he doesn't have time for it. The box by his feet and the pain in his back – the pigeon bites are sore, the fear has its taste. His cracked lips and croaked words –

Hello, he says. He manages.

My family, Jan tells him. Welcome. Here you see all of what we have. He points to brown sacks in a corner. There, potatoes. My mushrooms. He points to a bucket in another. There, toilet. Of course I help. He points to a cabinet. Television, VCR. He points to the ceiling. The old hotel Premier Inn. We are in her. Safer. You will have gun.

And fish man, Jan says. My wife will look your back now.

She looks on, vexed by this fish man in wet wool and tarp.

Then you rest, Jan tells Brian. Rest until we find you chair.

Jan's wife seems torn between submission and fright. Her husband's will is her way – but more than that, it's the gentleness of her touch; the lightness of the sponge across Brian's back. His broad back, sagging at the flanks, with a little definition and lots of bad skin.

His jumper to his side. His heart through his ears.

She draws the sponge from shoulder to spine, and out. Drawing wide V-shapes, chevrons, down his back. Into a bucket and on to his skin.

Down to the pain – the stripe in the centre, right along the spine, equidistant from the lumbar bones and the nape.

She teases wool fibres from the wound, and the wound is a welt. The six-inch line is weeping plasma. It's raised at least a half-centimetre.

She pulls lint from the wound, sticky and sore. It feels good, and Brian feels the tingle, lost in it, not questioning a thing. A pressure sore, maybe. From the chair or the floor. The effort or the strain. He's rocked over on himself, the meat of him covered in plastic. His arms drawn over his nipples. The tingle down there, in his private parts, some feeling coming back.

It feels like a bruise, not that he'd know.

He winces, then. The edge of the sponge pulled over the last inch, and sore. He hisses. She pulls the sponge away. He cocks his head, waiting for prognosis, diagnosis, some sort of bleak news.

But she's crying –
What's the matter?
Sobbing her heart out –
What is it? What's the matter?

Backing away –

Tell me! Where's a bloody mirror in this hole?

He turns, side to side, side to side. The room spinning.
She comes round to his front –

Jan!

She traces a cross over her bosom –

Jan!

She places her hands on his shoulders –

You are possessed, she tells Brian. You do not touch
my children.

The sounds of Paris '69, of Manchester 2012, ring through
the car park, ring off the wet walls. The damp night and
the cold breeze, the wind with teeth. Outside, vehicles
are overturned; the chants are loud as the bottles find
their marks.

All night, the whole way through, and into tomorrow,
today, a full twelve hours of dissolving order and
demolition. A lot of hate and a lot more fear. Blood and
pavements. Twelve hours. Time rewound and left to
play. A long player, this one – the city caught by its short
and curlies.

A long player.

Brian sleeps on and off, on and off, and his dead
weight never seemed heavier. His aches and pains, aches
and groans.

Jan's kids don't sleep. Jan's kids have questions.

Daddy says the brown people hate our country, the
littlest says. The littlest in his duffel, who keeps fingering
his nose. Do they?

That's not true, goes Brian. Everybody hates this country. But you must love this country in spite –

Daddy says we had a bus.

The kids have their dropped vowels, their strange

169

hodge-podge accents. Local accents with Polish flecks. Dropping the vowels, changing thee to dee. Probably educated at one of the few schools worth trying. Where you pay or pull in favours to get your name on the register. That or one of them tunnel schools you hear about. Jan mentioned the tunnels – you have to put two and two together.

Did you see his bands?

Bands?

Jan's littlest pushes his duffel coat sleeve up his arm. There are eight black rubber bracelets. The kid waves it under Brian's nose.

How many lines you got? he whispers.

Lines? Brian shrugs. Brian only knows white lines on flat hard surfaces. I don't know –

I can't wait for my first real lines, Jan's littlest says. My father's got forty-two. Says he'll get a full-sleeve before he's dead.

You'll regret a tattoo, Brian tells him.

Do you want to play a game?

I don't know any games.

We have a talker. We talk to our friends on it. You can play –

Brian shrugs.

It's over there. You press the button and say hello and sometimes they say hello as well.

Walkie-talkies?

Jan's littlest shakes his head. The hair mats and sticks across his forehead.

A radio? Is that it?

A talker, Jan's littlest says. Come see.

I can't move, Brian tells him. All this dead weight and weighty dread.

Oh.

170

Where's your father now?

On a mission, the child tells Brian.

Brian shakes his head. He can't be out there, in that, in and among that.

And your mother?

Jan's littlest shrugs. Sleeping I think.

Okay, Brian says. I'm going to sleep now, too.

But you said you'd play a game.

No, lad – I said I don't know any.

Jan's littlest pulls a face.

I have another one here, he says. He pulls out a roll of Sellotape. What you do is find the end, stick a sheet to the wall, tighten the end up, close your eyes and spin it on the floor, and then you find the end again. If you are fast, you win! My mother's record was two seconds because she kept her fingernails long. That's what she told me.

Brian eyebrows go up.

I don't have any nails, he says.

Jan's littlest furrows his brow.

Is that because you are the devil?

Over the carpets, the patterns and fabric tigers, the vibrant bushes and the fraying edges, the room's edges – the edges of hospitality, where warm feet would land on cold grit – comes a jangling, jarring rattle.

Brian has learnt a new reflex. His hand goes to the handle. The box moves towards him.

The rattle's nuances, the sounds at top frequency, the spat-out grit, reach the far drape. The drape shifts. The rattle appears. A varnished wooden chair, set on hard rubber wheels, big foot plates on it, and backed with pale straps, being pushed by a sweating man.

Jan comes off the concrete and over the smooth. The

chair runs silent, its bearings in decent shape, to the mattress. To Brian's pit.

The man with antiques like my potato, Jan says.

Brian has heard of these collectors; these finders and keepers. Like him, his archives, they try and guard what happened before.

I take sack of potato and tell him mother has broke back, Jan continues.

Dead flash that, Brian says, looking it up and down. It's a beautiful thing.

It come with slope for entry and escaping, Jan tells him. It good solid wood.

You're decent, you are, Brian says.

You want try? I ask for big one.

I'll have a go, aye. Help me up.

Those hands go under those pits. Up he goes. Up and in. From unfolded to folded up.

On first impressions, the back of the chair is hard. The kind of hard that gives you decent posture or breaks your pelvis first. He finds that the back of the chair puts an even pressure on his welt; his worsening wound.

Brian's mashed feet sag into the foot plates. It fits real nice. It fits pretty good. It fits, and no less.

Fish man can breathe once again, Jan tells Brian, and points to his back. Do you want squashing behind here?

Brian shakes his head.

Pressure's good, ta.

Because the pressure spreads the pain thin.

Good, says Jan. Now you stay and have time for practise. I go again.

The old CB unit has a lot of character, if that's what you call dents. The children handle it with that enthusiasm you lose at puberty. They point out the dials, the needles, the receiver cord and the sprouting wires. Brian pretends to care. Nods when he thinks he's meant to. But his ears prick when the static flares; when the first few voices cut across.

Jesus, Brian says – just as he realises Jan must have tapped the city mains. This works?

In a huddle, they're sweeping for decent signals, chatty channels. Usually settling on the city's unofficial channel twelve. The crackle and the waves as the bands swap seats with static.

Ears on? What's that handle, big boy?

Brian swallows.

Anybody?

I'm . . . I'm Meredith.

Roger that, Meredith. Call me what you like, though others get away with Merc, but said Merk, like merkin but chopped in half. You come over noisy that way, pal.

War outside, isn't it.

Got eyeballs on my own war, the man says. My war at home. Where are you?

Long since left. I'm staying with friends.

Oh aye?

Yes.

Quiet mouse are we? I'm in this dusky husk they called Tameside once upon a time. Bunker life's easy in't it, when you know how. Got me telly, got me auto-feeder, got me united re-runs. You there, big boy?

Yes.

Mint. So whereabouts you hiding now? Don't we all ask that on first dates? Sense of place in't it.

Brian swallows.

Bloody atmosphere's blue up here.

Pure bear patrols, is why pal? Caught the arse-end of news before. All kicking off again.

Sounds like they've got the pigs out, aye.

All the same, these bleedin' protesters. How I see it is they don't know what they want or why they're 'aving it in the first place. Browns on whites on whites on browns. Tellin' you mate. Weird. If it in't the government it's their mates in job queue. They don't bomb shit. It's the councils. Same old fear, divide and conquer and all that, in't it?

Maybe –

Trust, mate. Trust me. You think they're, even arsed about us lot down 'ere, in these shitholes with twenty quid for a month or whatever?

I don't know.

Civil war's good for 'em innit? S'what they want. Get all these bad scrotes off the streets, they're thinking. Dunno what they fuckin' expect turning off our footy anyways. No porn, no footy, no fuckin' wife to speak of. No wonder all these mad-head white-boys start making bombs and fightin' pakis all over. And the pakis themselves. You aren't a paki are you Meredith?

Brian doesn't say much. Doesn't say anything to that.

Where was you again, mate?

Near Victoria station.

No way, Merc says. Speak to kids that way on some nights, me.

Brian looks at Jan's firstborn.

Yeah?

Aye, precocious buggers an' all. Pair of 'em, till their mam gets on the mic as well.

Brian is staring at Jan's children.

Their dad's some assassin, mind. Won't be fuckin' with that.

Assassin?

Oh aye. These kids of his got their own gun stash for

when he's out. They've had it rattling about when I've been on before. Mental –

Brian has stopped listening. Brian has basically stopped breathing –

And he freelances for these Wilbers, Merc says. Nob-'eads them mate; another bunch you don't see pulling weight for new lands and glory.

Thought you said you were in a bunker, says Brian.

Bunker with a fuckin' massive aerial on it, aye. Anyway mate. Just keep your head down in there. Won't be like 2012 till army turns in, so you've got a couple of days holding on yet. Got a mate broadcasting out of some squat in the Ferguson if you need more local news. Better view than many he's got up there. Want the frequency?

Brian nods as if it's obvious. Brian distant. Brian speaks: Go on.

But those bad words are ringing.

Wilber. Freelancer.

The boat rolling past their camp.

The wife and her fear.

The children and their dirty, filthy fingernails.

So Brian drops the mic. Backs away. The kids take note and get on with their games. Their chats and their check-ins.

The whole world is too good to be true.

The run is a roll and his way to the light.

The concrete and the stairs and out for the night –

The chair is weighty, Colin's box doubly so, and the ramp of the car park is hard.

The kids are unconscious. Bruises at worst. Not a proud moment. Not a bloody proud moment from any angle.

His shaking hands beneath the still-wet wool, scrab-

175

bling about in the only pockets that count. The pockets for spare fifties and the two vital business cards. Wet, they're wet, but not all gone. He squints, doesn't he. Squints to see a pair of names, the streaking numbers.

Tariq.

Ian.

Brian stole matches, too. He has matches. He stole fruit; he has apples. He has the box –

Jan's wife was sleeping. Drugged, maybe, the more you think on it.

Jan on his errands; bombing about in these unsociable hours. And Brian keeps running, rolling. Not knowing the day. The days gone, his house gone, Diane –

The dirty pavement, these filthy roads, the markings rubbed off and the grids filled and emptying themselves. Manchester, his Manchester — as sharp on the eyes as any broken bottle.

Brian hangs some corners and rattles along, the box in his lap like some anchor. He's got everything wrong.

He stops by the river, facing the cathedral. The city's Godhead. And from so many spire tips, God looks back down on everything. If he's real, he won't miss a trick. The coke in the towers; the lives of His flowers.

BUT HE ISN'T LISTENING.

Brian, he says sorry just in case. He lights a match and tosses it over the bridge. He can't see the water, but hopes the rainbow-oil will set alight.

He moves along, then. When nothing happens. When he doesn't even hear the fizz. He moves on towards town, and smoke. Towards orange-bottomed clouds and the screams and the firebombs.

And it's funny, you know. He's not used to the wheelchair's rattles. The hardness of the wheels themselves.

176

But he likes it. The pain of his back spread out flat.

From balconies and roads round corners, he can hear shouting. A black hole pulling their city back in. And Brian has the box, the chair, but no plans.

All around, rubber smoke, that barricade cologne, hangs over everything. Something hotter, nastier, tickles his septum. Tear gas already.

It takes just a moment longer to notice:

The Beetham Memorial Column is off.

Brian whispers his mother's tongue:

I beheld the earth. And, lo, it was waste and void. And the heavens, they had no light.

And morning has broken with rubber bullets.

Brian has a pair of business cards. Cards where the ink ran but the numbers held. Salvation is a bunch of fifties he keeps for emergencies. Fifties for payphones and cig papers. Fifties he's found. This is it. This is the phone box. He fights the door open. And his hands are on the back panel of the phone box, fully out of his seat now. The cards of the Cat Flap in every frigging call box in this city. His back lighting up, sharp and hot, and all this sweat in his eyes.

So the coins go in. He pecks out the first set of digits. The heat and sweat, the stinging cheeks and blood-shot eyes.

Tariq dials out.

Tariq dials out twice.

He pecks out Ian's number.

Ian dials out.

Brian pecks out his home number – holding his breath.

50p in. Ring ring.

Ring ring.

Ring ring.

Ring ring.

Hello, Brian.

Are you Jesus? Brian says.

No, Ian says. Why? Are you?

I'm Neptune, Brian says. And soon as I get chance I'm coming to rip your head off.

This was the wrong street. It was the worst street. It was the street between –

One lad lumps Brian in the face. Another wraps Saint George's flag round his head and twists the ends, squashing his nose. More punches fall in. The heel of a boot in the groin.

The fuck is your legs about man, one of them says. Through all of it, Brian holds that box for dear life.

Pigs! shouts this other. Down there!

Brian can't see much for the cut on his eyebrow. He can hear the pig, though. Everyone can hear the tracks, the whistling. It's a tank, after all. A tank for coppers.

Fucking do one boys! this lad says. Their footsteps cobble the road. They try tipping Brian's chair for good measure –

Brian pulls away with the flag. He half-sees the pig roll up. It's Tiananmen Square all over. The brakes peal. The top hatch pops. Some council goon has his head out, his war-face on. A camera hanging off his helmet.

You escaped a care home have you?

Enjoying the fresh air, Brian says, his hand turned a shiny red. He mops his eyes with the flag. Leave me be.

Curfew's extended, smart-arse. You're meant to be inside. We can haul you in if needs be.

I'm on my way, Brian tells him. Just passing through.

You're advised to listen to Council radio for the time being. Get yourself out of harm's way.

No need to shout at me –

The council goon shakes his head and gets on with his work. Brian sits in the exhaust fumes as the pig trundles past.

Brian in his chair in the centre of his dying city.

Brian pets his forehead, his lump. He wipes his eyes clear again. He gets his bearings. Looks this way and that.

He spots something. He starts to laugh.

On the wall, to his right, on dented shutters, in baby-pink paint-spray –

THE DEVIL MAKES WORK FOR IDLE HANDS.

Past a bathroom shop, its shutters only half down; a chippy with its windows done in, a hollowed out, drained-flat bookies; an empty chapel-booth; all these places closed for a bad sort of national holiday. The curfew like some tide that pulls away and leaves the courageous or the stupid outside.

On down the road through the ash and embers.

Bathroom shop.

And back. The guilt – the excitement – the buzz – the single-mindedness of a special kind of bastard –

The window goes in, just like that. Big plate glass bugger as well, floor to ceiling. Brian curses the day they glazed it; makes a pig's ear of the shards and splinters. Still: your man goes in. Nowt comes out. Your man just rolls in.

The alarm fires up the second he's all through. Roars into his lugs. It stops all thought except the critical ones. Thoughts going: Water. Salt. Bath.

He gets it sorted. A good old rummager for all his faults. Getting used to the chair, now, too – the chair and how far you can lean out of it. And the back door's lock

179

is bust. So he's out and in the yard. There's a bin of it, water, very tepid and kind of brown. Out in the yard, the loading area, with the empty cages and polystyrene; the plastic wrap and the cardboard piles.

It takes about three weeks to drag it through at any rate. These legs of his, aren't they a pain. But he does it, our Brian. Somehow he drags the bin of water inside. He has to on account of it's worth it. Because it usually is.

There's salt in the kitchen, as well. All this with the alarm still going. It's too high to reach when he clocks it; rifling the cupboards and smashing pots and mugs and plates around him. Bloody mayhem all things considered. And there – top shelf. Sundries and that. The lo-salt in the red pot. So he goes at that with a mop, swiping like some blind swordsman. He brings the lot down. Oh aye, there's the salt.

Salt for a bath.

He lies on his own in that dark showroom, the salted water lapping over his toes, his penis afloat, the water turned pink, and the world buzzes on, turns on its axis, swings heavy round the sun. Nobody can see him, because the shutters are up and the glass is broken, same as anywhere else – and come on, why would you want to loot a frigging bathroom shop besides – but he can see out; see the pavements picked out in bad light; the police and protesters running and stopping, closing and brawling, falling and screaming. Nightsticks in, blood out, boots in, teeth out.

And God, were He real and listening, God looks down from His perch, His cathedral seat, His temple suite.

And God sighs. His sons and servants warring.

16.

On his way to nowhere, down these bloodied roads, Brian sees this patrol lev come in low. It arcs in from a good hundred yards on the diagonal, planing through riot smoke. It skates on its air-brakes, and stops, hissing exhaust fumes. Brian can hear the motors crackling static. Brian tucks himself into a shop front, moving pretty quick all told. The pigs in the lev have words with their walkie-talkies – Brian can hear whatever control's barking back. Then one throws his legs out the door and drops the earthing cord.

They aren't arsed about Brian, don't notice – there's a mashed body a little farther down the street. Its legs are bent up the wrong way, and the chunks –

They pick up the body. Leastways it comes off whole. They roll it into a bag, a sack, and drag that sack back to the lev, still purring away. The council pigs hook up the sack to lev.

Into walkie-talkies goes some mention of RTAs.

A large, heavy vehicle seems to have collided with a civilian, they say. They're smirking. They're getting the giggles –

When they notice Brian watching.

The walkie-talkies go away. Council boys become the heavy-set thugs in big bad boots.

Past everyone's bed time now, the biggest says. You won't want to mention this, will you mate?

Brian shakes his head.

There's a good boy.

And next time, says the other, you just tell your grubby comrades to look both ways before our boys roll through.

Pig, Brian says.

What's that now?

A new question: how do you detain a man in a wheel-chair? The answer is you don't. The answer is tie him to the chair with a bloodied Saint George's flag and hope nobody sees.

Nobody sees.

Not often you get a decent view of a place on fire. Not often at all. Brian gets his served with a motor block under his arse; the rear bench diamond-hard, his new wheelchair banging off his fused knees every time the lev banks to turn. And it banks a lot.

From above, Manchester's council building is a lumpen thing of Yorkshire stone; a fat triangle only yards from the blackened husk of central library. You miss the details and the flourishes – the statues and the carving. They pass bar-ricades and smoke plumes, a kilometre of sharpline from pillar to post. Like Normandy's beaches, it is.

A fence of pigs has closed the roads, the entrances, on either side, and there's a half-circle of half-tracks on Albert Square in front. Nobody's getting in, but burning tyres says they've tried. Brian spots sentries – mainly on the pillar-tops; between the goth-y decorations; and one up the bell tower. They carry big rifles for their civic du-ties; civic duties in trying times. They're taking pot-shots at pigeons down on the square.

Brian's heard stories about this place.

You can't strong-arm a man in a wheelchair, but these boys make an admirable go of it. He's in a narrow lift downwards, given short thrift. A network of corridors in the glass-fronted hive. The colony in white shirts, in ties. From the view, Brian guesses at a third floor, maybe the fourth. Too high for heroics. The gentlemen from the council don't say much at all. To a desk with a scratched wooden top; a counter, with sheet-steel slats. Their budgets go here –

Brian's nose is bleeding. Airbrakes, they'll get you like that.

Some hard face comes over. PC Plod in a riot visor – these men in funny hats.

This bloody spazz in for?

Curfew section ten. Abusing a council member.

PC Plod shakes his head.

Very grave, he says. Name?

Brian tells him.

I said, Name.

Brian tells him louder.

Address.

Brian lies while PC Plod takes notes.

Bought my last trainers back there, me –

Brian says nothing.

Do you smoke, Brian?

What?

Do you?

Yeah.

Drugs?

No.

PC Plod smiles. PC Plod takes a sheet of A4 from the office printer. He looks at his officers.

And clean this bugger's mush, will you? Just polished us floors.

The men listen and obey –

So what we putting you down as? Mujahid? National-ist? Wilber?

Brian's turn to laugh.

Slap-head of yours says the middle one.

Brian and his shaved head –

You understand that you've been detained, Mr Mer-edith. I mean men your age should know better.

Brian doesn't know where to start.

You'll be processed in the morning, PC Plod says, pull-ing out a plastic tray. Put your possessions in this.

Look, I were just out and about –

In curfew hours? When we're out trying to stop world war bleeding three?

I need to keep this box, Brian says. I'm an unwell man.

With what?

With life.

Well, you're keeping nothing, sunshine. Put your things in here – won't ask you again.

I have to keep the box.

Why, what's up with you?

It doesn't have a name, what I've got.

PC Plod looks at his colleagues again. His eyebrows up.

Put this fucking idiot to sleep, he says. To Brian: Box on here. Now.

The box doesn't fit in the tray.

You don't want to look in there, says Brian.

They don't listen. Nobody listens. They start to wheel Brian along. To the bank of cells in the guts of this castle. Brian starts to laugh again –

Then have a good bloody gander inside, you bastard! Brian shouts back. A good bloody look at yourself!

PC Plod, the voice in Brian's ear, he says, Got a special cell for you, lad.

Past others, crying through their bars, holy books and tissue on the floor in bits in the spaces between. Blood on walls. Halfway down, there's a T-junction. Dark corridors and men – and they are mostly men – with bad hearts. Down they go, right to the end, another right. No crumbs, no, but that minotaur is waiting –

Here, the pig says. Right special cell, is yours. No windows or bars, but plenty of cushioning.

The bolts, the joints, the reinforced hinge and –

The black.

PC Plod says, Sleep tight, sweetheart.

17.

It is stifling black; black as the hole he fell out of. The smell of sewers, the crushing space. Brian has fallen a little farther down the rabbit-hole.

His eyes adjust, taking in the dimensions. His eyes scurry and run from his head. He's meant to take breaths, to calm himself. Like if the bombs fell for real and you got trapped.

But through the dark, there's something. He can't calm down. Over there, in the corner. An outline you recognise with more attention; hard-wired in there, a shape written on the insides of your skullcase. Another human, the organic shape of round shoulders. Brian waves his hands about.

Hello? he says.

But the figure is still, too still. So Brian hesitates. Brian waits to see if there's any movement. The sounds of ventilation ducting and heavy fans. Shouting from inside, shouting from out. He goes closer. The figure is straining, restrained – the breath all comes through his nose.

And the pigs – PC Plod and his pigs elsewhere in their grey-stone palace. The pigs, they say, Let there be light, and there is, and all in these cells are blinded by halogen panels. And the police are dead chuffed because everyone screams. And Brian sees everything, through that screaming light, the flash of it, just that second.

The lights reveal padded walls with thick, roped seams.

And the gag on this man – the packing-tape mask. The chin is shiny-wet. The floor's soiled between the tyres.

Back to black.

Brian feels out for the person, his heart in his hands. Their hands are bound, this person's. Another man in another chair. He stirs at Brian's touch. The figure says it, Mmff, like that, Mmff, again, and the eyes open and the straining starts hard. Straining against the handles and the strapping.

Calm down, for crying out loud, Brian says. Shush man, they'll hear you. I'll open it up –

The flash sears again in the special padded room.

Brian frees the boy's hands; pulls the tape off this wet mouth. There's a sock in there. The man's not a man, a boy. The unmistakable face of a person with Down's Syndrome. His wide eyes full with fear.

What did you do, son? What did they do you for?

Brian guesses at his age – guesses at seventeen. The kid is trembling, wiping his face where the tape went. Spitting, trying to pull fibres off his tongue. Our Christ, Brian says. Because the world has accelerated again.

Lights out.

The boy grips Brian's hand. The boy holds Brian's hand in his own, in both of his cold, clammy hands, and pulls Brian's arm around his neck. He pushes his face to Brian's collar, slobbering across his neck and shoulder. Dog breath and body odour. Brian, he pats the boy's back. Come on, big fella, don't be crying like this –

The boy, in this cell of theirs, with the padded walls. Their faces as lines scratched onto black wax, lit so softly by a crack under the door. The boy says, stuttering, Superman.

They come in to say their bit with bright torches in their faces. The Down's Syndrome boy is screaming, so they

187

wheel him out of the cell and leave him to entertain the corridor.

They stand Brian out of his chair. They put a knee in the crux of his own. He crumples. They laugh a lot about that. They get him back up again. They pull him into his chair and towards a cold wall. They say, Out. Feet there. Put your filthy hands out on there. Stretch those fingers out. Spider them. Go on. Good, that's it. Now lean forward. He leans forward, gingerly, slow. And they time it, they count. He doesn't last long – they get to forty-five.

He falls to his knees – his knee, whatever you want to call it. His blood is the warmest thing in the room. They slap him to shock, never to bruise. Not that anybody will care. They slap him some more.

Up – come on. On the wall again. Go on, you fucking lug. Get them feet spread. But he can't, can he, on account of he doesn't have feet. So they kick him square in the backside.

Right up the jacksy, they say to him. You love things up your arse, don't you, you filthy little prick.

They work out fast that his back is sore. They put truncheons to it – position them like chisels. And they pretend their hands are hammers. They give their truncheons a tap, then a slap. They laugh when he screams. They laugh when they run their truncheons up and down the wound, through his clothes. When they poke his anus with their truncheons and ask if he likes it.

Re-education through hurting, they tell him. See this as a corrective labour camp.

Brian asks for painkillers and gets a look.

The banging and thumping carries on outside. The screaming streets of Manchester.

They're pulling our city down.

188

Brian cannot sit or lie. Can't get comfy on his side nor on his back. The bruises are lumps, his skin turned to paper. And the wound in his back is a running tap – the sticky interstitial fluid is bonding him with his clothes.

Alone in the dark with a single blanket. He's man without his night lamp; his North Star hidden by bad, black clouds. Filthy cheeks against the cold floor.

He says something over and over. Another one of his mother's:

The end of that man is peace.

The bloody hell is that smell? is how they start his morning. To him, Brian that is, the days have pushed up against each other without a seam. And they look on this pile of a person, our Brian, on his floor. Two kinds of bastard hovering over him.

Wake up, treasure, they say to him. You're in the hot seat.

Brian wakes like that. To the padded walls and their terrible stains. The quiet of a whole wing sedated, the ducting still crackling above. His back's on fire; really bad now. He's read about this kind of injury –

He catches the smell, too. Gags before his eyes go full-saucer.

No, he says, coughing up those famous morning lumps.

What even is that? says PC Plod.

Smell of captivity in't it, the other guy goes. The razor wit. Bung a man in a room like this, he wakes up reeking like tinned fucking tuna. Had a bad turn, have you?

You letting me off? Brian asks.

The pigs turn together and turn back, laugh together at some private gag.

Slight change of plan. We've things to talk about – sure you'll understand.

Brian puts the back of his hand to his back wound. It comes away wet and sticky. The lump was a half-inch thicker; harder by a factor of plenty. The fish smell is actually unbearable. And dizziness takes its host.

Ten minutes play like a bad montage. In and out, play, pause, play. The rooms spliced by closing his eyes, the sweat pouring off him, stinging his eyes. Through to an interview room, oval, two-way mirrors, made in the image of an interview room. Just like the films. Here on his arse for the same old questions. Two men and a table. A table and a recording tablet.

Who are you working for what's your ideology we'll do a lie detector test.

And the answers:

Nobody I don't have one I've nothing to lie about.

You'd better fill us in you'd better not lie you'd better tell us everything.

I don't know what you want.

Okay. Have a think on that one.

The coppers stand up and leave the room.

Owing to three hours alone, Brian could tell you about every last surface. The way the table has warped, the dodgy plastering over dark stains, the dents in the concrete fill floors. The heel marks on varnished wood, the rusting joints on chairs. Hell, he could have counted the tiles of the suspended ceiling, the time he's been on his own here. Because, you see, that's how they've played him today.

We're not inhuman, they said with a wink. Only

they've holed him up good; left him with a chunk of mossy bread and a dog bowl of off-white milk.

The coppers come back.

As he sits, one of the men goes, Lad sat there once, he was, and he shat all over the place. Terrible mess.

He asks his esteemed colleague, Remember that?

Oh aye, hard to forget.

And that lad with the hair – remember?

Puddled our floor, him. Didn't have to lift a finger. Think he confessed to something he couldn't have done just to get into Strangeways and out of here.

Brian is swaying, side to side. Three hours alone, not a place to hide.

And not to forget that slag on her knees –

Oh no. Never forget that one, will we –

So hard to –

But we've given you a bit of time now, Brian. So would you like to tell us why you were out on our streets, after the watershed?

You got nothing better to do than this with people who can't even walk?

Don't play that card, you fat little cretin.

I just don't see –

And the box – tell us about that box. 'Cause since our man on reception had himself a nosey, he's gone home with a green face and terribly loose bowels.

I told him not to look in there, Brian says. I told you all. Are you going to let me go or what?

One of the men reaches down. One at a time, he produces a twenty-deck of cigarettes, a full ashtray, and an old pint pot, filled with water. He arranges all three on the desk.

You're not scared of us, are you? 'Cause see, you're loyal to your King, but not the law of your country.

Done nowt wrong, have I, Brian says. What's to be scared of?

I think you're confused – we've processed enough like you. Tell us who you're affiliated with, and we might cut a deal. Difficult for us to monitor without the web, the mobiles, isn't it? 'Cause if you listen out there it's the skinheads doing half the damage.

One of the men stands up, stretches out. He paces wall to wall. He settles behind Brian.

The seated copper picks up the fags.

Smoke? You smoke, don't you?

I'm all right.

Go on, son. You look right peaky.

Brian hesitates. The copper nods, smiles. Brian takes a cigarette. It takes six tries to spark it up. He pulls the ashtray towards him. That smell of old cigs. The crushed butts and the black rim.

Look Brian, says the man behind him. We'd really love to know about your box.

Told you. You don't look in it. I'm just minding it for someone.

So why don't you look in it?

You just don't.

The seated man pours the ashtray into the pint pot. The man behind Brian knocks the cigarette from his hand; armlocks him.

The seated man stirs the ash through the water. The pint has turned a ninja black.

So, tell us about your legs then. Tell us about that instead –

Brian squirms, the tears hot in his eyes.

No –

192

Oh come on, treasure. No need for crocodile tears. We're just looking out for you.

I don't get what you're on about –

The seated man stands up. The man behind pulls Brian's head back and pincers his nose.

Sure you don't want to tell us?

Brian cries out –

The rancid water goes over his face. Brian's head is held still, his eyes closed, choking and coughing and retching. The smell is vile –

Drink up lad, the man pouring his pint says. We'll try again tomorrow.

And in that dark, dark cell, there was a dark, dying man.

And the smell, that reeking tuna-can smell, it gets worse all night, or maybe all day. Dead, rotten fish. Dead, suppurating skin. The skin of old, left to soak.

Sometimes, you can get used to a smell. You adjust to it and don't remember till someone else points it out. Not this one. The air's so thick he gags. This one wakes him up, eventually. And he is lying in a slick. It's an oil slick – in the bad light, it's that black.

He panics. Could be blood. He checks his wounds, checks his face, his anus, the holes in his goddamned breaking heart.

Nothing.

But the smell. The smell and the taste.

He tries to get back to sleep. If a pig will roll its own mess –

And in that dark, dark cell.

There was a monster.

The morning after the war before, it's like they can smell it too. That's why they burst in with masks on their faces, bad things on their minds. And the men from the council scream in Brian's face – about the rotten smell and the black, shiny mess around him.

Get hose out the store cupboard, one shouts to the other. For God's sakes.

If you can't get up to take a piss, you don't get your shower, he barks at Brian.

And sooner than he's come round, they're blasting him, clothes and all. Pushing Brian up against the back wall of his cell – black water rolling off him in waves; lapping the skirting and soaked up by the padding. Still in his clothes; from shallow sleep to awake and screaming. His wheelchair turned over.

Brian slips, slides, tries to get up and in his chair. A sorry creature whose dignity comes with sitting down. That awful fishy smell on all fronts – the black liquid getting soaked into the walls.

They blast his hands off the wood; aim for his eyes and crotch.

They go for his mouth, his nose.

Choking, choking, suffocating pressure.

Till his lungs are breaking, groaning –

And he has to breathe, take in the water. The water flashes across his lungs. It burns and tears and ruptures.

But he does not cough or drown or move.

He sits there. And he takes it. He breathes. He breathes the water they turn over his smashed body.

Eventually the water runs clear – the cell's back wall turned a uniform grey. And the pigs stop laughing, get bored, don't realise. So they slap him raw for ten minutes instead. A good cuffing round the earholes for their troubles. The nasty sting of hands striking wet skin.

Brian's heavy and sodden. He's cold and wheezing. But he could breathe –

He points at the hose, holding his tiger-striped face. Do it again, he says, laughing. Go on, you bloody animals. Do it with more salt.

The coppers drag Brian through and set him up for a grilling. Same two council men, in the interview room, with the same old questions:

Who are you working for? What's your ideology? What's in that box? We'll do a lie detector test.

And get the exact same answers:

Nobody. I don't have one. I don't know. I've nothing to lie about.

All the very same – the ash tray and a pint; the fag he can't smoke because he can't even think of it.

Go back to bed, they tell him. Brian holding his face, the smell of tar all around. And they rewind their tablet, play back the words, laugh, and scrub them forever.

Anyway, Brian sleeps through this time. His body aches too much to notice what happens with the lights out and the battles outside.

When he wakes up, it's to a dreadful pain in his armpits. His first reaction is to rub them, but it hurts too much – sharp and sore, like a spot caught under the skin. Instead, he pushes his hands up his jumper and fingers his armpits, gently, a lightness you might find ticklish. He finds the skin has gone baggy and loose. It jolts him upright. It's a new horror. He wipes his face on wet wool.

Panicking, he fingers the lines, these new contours. He pushes fingers along the fleshy channels – still very sore if he presses too hard. Warm grooves cut out of his body.

He clutches his fused thighs. Where the lateral contact between each limb is at its most seamless. It feels harder than usual. He wants to be sick and nearly is. He lifts the blankets. The light touch here now. And the skin's definitely turned harder. There's a sort of carapace around the withered muscle. No, he whispers. No . . .

He lifts the blanket, forces himself to look. In this light, the skin's the colour of scab; it's turned crusty and weeping where his knee joint has bent. Writhing now, as though it burns, Brian begins to sweat – the tuna smell coming from every pore of his body. His own self has turned alien, turned abject. He's half a man with not much left at all.

He has transformed. He's transforming –

Pinch yourself, he thinks. Just pinch yourself.

But it's simple fascination with horror, this time. Because he's found lesions in his armpits. Neat, open lines, working across his skin. And there are hard, golden-brown scales and scabs spread across these malformed limbs.

Gills and scales, he thinks, remembering his myths. Meat.

It's the box.

He shakes his head.

What happened to Noah, those wings on the floor.

He strokes his fresh armour –

The edges of the scabs. The give in his skin.

It's how you see yourself. Your hard-wiring, blown up into sight.

These lesions that yawn and ripple.

Your hopes and fears; your darkness and dreams.

Fresh lungs and holes and ways to breathe.

The box is a mirror.

That worm in the apple has been drawn with my bite.

Last chance saloon, the coppers tell Brian, squatting over the pitted floor. Brian is leaning on his wooden chair, drawing laboured breaths, the chair vibrating on account of his shivers.

They've brought a holdall bag. One of them is tossing and catching a corkie cricket ball.

In these end-times, they tell him, it's dead common for the fearful to turn to the King of Kings. You'll know about that, won't you? Man of your type. Still. Peculiar how the Lord God our Saviour has become a best pal to all these up and down these cells. Oh aye, we've heard all that as well. On the streets, they want something to cling to. Death in your face puts a new spin on your faith. So are you going to repent?

For what? Brian says. Brian means.

Make yourself feel better, won't it.

You don't even know what you want from me.

They put the bag down. They have an ashtray and a checker-board rag.

Lady Law says we get to keep you. And yeah, we have an idea.

What?

We've got Wilber friends who'll put you to better use, even if we can't glean a bit of intelligence out of your fat skull.

They hold him down. They pull out clothes. Cricket whites, of all things.

Thought we'd play a great British sport today, they say. Or is it your bunch, your skin-heads, who call these garrison games? Distractions from the truth. Pursuits that mask the pursuits of others.

I don't –

They grab Brian's face. Let's get you changed for a nice game of cricket.

They wipe ash all over his face so his face is black. S'get you nice and ready.

197

And they wheel him outside. Down the cells, the corridor of doors.

The varnished floor doesn't take any speed from the ball. It skips, just like a flat stone spun fast over a calm lake, and smashes into the wall next to Brian. The tiles spray grey dust.

Prisoners are screaming, cheering, rattling their cages.

Brian watches the ball roll back along the corridor. His hands are bound tight behind his back, his head tilted forward to save his face. It would be easier not to watch – but every time PC Plod goes to bowl, his pal rallies him for the shot.

Ooh! he goes, like it's a real match.

So the varnished floor doesn't take any speed from the ball. This time, it skips short, and bounces hard. This time, it takes Brian in the gut, and folds him over.

LB! shouts the bowler.

His friend, PC Plod, raises his finger.

A fine wicket, he says.

The noise starts to rouse more prisoners, most of whom can't see what's happening. More start yelling and banging on their doors – come the revolution, that kind of rubbish. Probably thinking the lads outside have gotten themselves in.

Then another ball, the third of this over. Deliberate and slow, so Brian can see where it's going to end up. It arcs in from a springy left hand, the seam a perfect horizontal. When it connects, it edges his throat – and Brian screams, chokes, struggling against the ropes.

Ooh, says PC Plod; the prisoners like a crowd commiserating a near-miss.

This is how you make them feel, PC Plod says. This is why they're rioting on your doorstep.

Brian coughs, coughs and spits on the floor.

You've got me so wrong.

No point being a nationalist no more, says PC Plod.

But I'm not a frigging nationalist, whispers Brian.

They bowl another.

I'm not a racist.

Another at him – the crack of his nose, this time. The blood up his face.

He comes at them. He uses his mushed-together feet to pull himself down the corridor –

Blood and tears and snot and salt; muck and black and spit and ash.

They bowl fast and low. An over. His forehead catches one –

Got your own bud-bud-ding-ding bruise now! shouts PC Plod.

Coming and going, swaying and rocking.

He's coming to get us! they shout.

Just kill me, says Brian, over the racket, rolling towards them using his smashed feet as leverage. Just do me in.

And they see that his tears are coming out black.

One of the policemen headlocks Brian – drags him on his toes and through to the interview room. The other plonks himself in Brian's wooden chair, mocking his movement, rattling and rolling in behind. And into the borderless space, where time stops and props come out and torment starts, they haul Brian up and dump him in the chair; throw a balled fist at his eyebrow for their trouble.

Stay still, says one.

Won't bail out of this round, says the other.

I don't know what you're looking for, Brian tries to say – his voice cracked now, his face grubby with ashtray foundation, streaked with dark tears.

A bit of no-strings fun.

In the two-way – the mirror hiding ghosts from another room – he catches his own gaze; the sallow cheeks and the cruel lines. Twin voids set in a haunted face; two white marbles set in a weather-worn tombstone.

See, half the buggers in here haven't seen the sun in months, Brian. They stopped screaming a long time back. We'd like to help you help yourself. We'd just like you to co-operate. Give us names, addresses. Because –

The copper has stopped. He asks the other: Did you hear that?

What?

Were that you? Knocking on the table?

Was it heck.

Brian shifts, fidgets.

The man starts again.

Where were we? Go on. What you got for us?

Brian snaps. Brian has a brainwave. Brian says: Person you want to go after lives out near Flouch roundabout. Ian. He's got lads down here – he's got heads on their way. Wants to pull some kind of coup – he's one of these Anglo-Saxon heritage lot. Total nutter. Totally insane. And he's got you –

Hang about, one of the coppers says, his hand up. Took me a while to work out where you were talking. Flouch roundabout? That's on the way to Sheffield lad. We haven't worked with West Yorkshire lot since the last riots. So let's maybe talk about people closer to home.

Brian shakes his head.

You don't understand, he says.

One of the coppers slams a fist to the table.

You don't understand. West Yorkshire isn't our scene. Isn't owt to do with any of us. How many Anglo-Saxon fans you think we see every week in this place? Crawl out their rocks, in their white masks, to cause a fuss over some lad or another. How many d'you think we've had sat there, and tell us about this nigger or this paki, this wog or this chink? How many d'you think we've hand-cuffed trying to string up some poor lad from a lamp post? We've seen it all pal. And I reckon by now you've realised we deal with all of you the same. No discrimination. No fucking mercy. Off to the Wilbers with half, the bin for the rest.

But he's taken my house –

The copper holds up a piece of paper.

Says here you're staying at a shoe shop in Ancoats.

I – I don't know.

Tell us something you do, then.

I don't –

He your boss, this Ian? Are you a grass, Meredith?

No, I'm –

This time, all three of them hear the raps – four sharp bangs from the hidden side of the two-way.

One copper stands up and scans his lot. If you looked closer, you'd see the hairs of his arm on their ends.

Who's in there? he says. At this bloody time?

Not a clue, the other says, his watch held up to his face in bafflement.

The standing copper puts his ear to the glass. Cups it nice and tight.

Three, sharp raps on the two-way glass.

The copper pulls off and falls back.

Bloody hell –

The copper tries the door. The door won't shift. The copper's hands are shaking.

The other copper stands up fast. Brian sways; eyes forward, thinking on the other side, of what can see all three.

A single, loud bang rattles the fixings.

The coppers together put their eyes to the glass.

Another. The coppers back away, swallowing hard. One of them slaps on the intercom, yells desperately at the radio fuzz.

The glass begins to sing. It vibrates in a low note. It hums, peals, and finally it splits. Small lines crawl out from a single point in its centre, cracks sluicing from the middle to its edges. The panel sags from the middle, its falling weight bringing the top foot or so with it. Brian recoils, shuts his eyes.

And PC Plod, times two, they're both on the floor.

Brian bends back, as far as this wooden spine will let him; the open welt searing hot, a pulse in his back, a network of pain lighting up with bruises for nodes.

The kind of screaming you don't forget. An over-powering smell – sweet, sticky, fecal. Brian recognises it as decay; dying cells and yellow fluids –

A stormcloud of flies comes through the hole and cycles the room. Bluebottles and sandflies and midges and horse flies, their buzzing in all frequencies, their legs on every surface.

In that day the Lord will whistle for flies, Brian thinks. Brian hears his mother say.

But nothing science or God could explain is beyond the smashed glass.

Before them, a near-naked creature cast in moon-white and gleaming – a twisted thing, its musculature worn inside-out, writhing skin torn over tubes of tendon, the skin flayed on its trunk, the skin stretched out across two-metre wings. And it shines, slick – gleaming wet with a kind of jelly. Hissing through the nose; the eyes forward.

In jerks, spasms, the creature comes at the interview room, grey powder loosed from the wings, shaken into thick air. These wings, heavy with this strange dust, crawl their way across the partition with the twitches of a wasp's antennae. Fully out, they stretch eight feet wall-to-wall. Pirate sails that hide the barren room behind.

The smell of it –

The bulk of this creature, this wet man-thing wreathed in dust, follows its wings. It bends into the frame, puts bare feet into the crystal mess. Brian catches a taser pulled out and primed, but the creature moves fast. Brian hears ribs go, the crack, sees arms turned and smashed against themselves. Through a ripped sleeve, he catches a glimpse of an old tattoo, suddenly warped and then ruptured by the snapped radius on its way through the skin, exploding into red.

The wet gurgle of a crushed throat, a rotten scream, these compound fractures pushed through crisp pleats in white shirts –

Oh God, oh God –

The flies on every surface watching and twitching – black-blue waves up every wall.

The creature rears back, its toothless grin, raw gums pulled tight. And it gleams, a film of something greasy, something that isn't sweat.

Brian, the man-thing says, in a rattle, its bubonic hand outstretched.

Brian replies with a name.

Not any more –

The creature smiles wider. Its wings collapse to its side –

I'm the angel of the fucking north, pal.

18.

Noah kicks the interview door clean from its frame. Pushes Brian along the corridors of men, mostly men, who cower in their cells or make threats in foreign tongues. The floors are slick with mucky footprints – un-wiped boots, rain, or worse. The smells shift with each metre; vomit turns to fear turns to stale. Some smells you wouldn't place; some you might mistake for infinitely nicer. Pair of them like some skewed version of Bonnie and Clyde, with blood on their clothes and filth under their nails.

They glide on through the town hall's fourth floor. The flies spread out in their wake.

They don't talk. They don't look.

Until:

Superman, Brian hears. A quiet whisper.

Brian sees the boy, his featureless face. His shiny, swollen cheek, this close to splitting open.

Stop, Noah, Brian says.

Noah stops. His big wings settle and shed dust like a pillow punched in a sunny room. The flies settle. The drone dims out.

Can we get him out?

Noah shakes his head.

He can't come with us. Not where we're going.

I'm not bloody asking that. Just to get the poor bugger out of that cell.

Noah leaves Brian where he is.

The kid has a string of spit swinging from his chin.

You'll be OK, son, Brian says.

You are dirty, the boy says.

I know.

I don't know where my mum lives.

You'll be OK, son.

The boy smiles – a bright smile marred by missing teeth.

Noah pads up the corridor – comes out of the black with his shredded, jelly-smeared face.

It's a circuit lock, he says. Open this one and I think they all go.

No, says Brian. It's a keycard lock – look.

But the cards are in the living quarters. I burnt everything –

Jesus bloody Christ, Noah.

Brian looks at the boy.

We can't leave him.

Noah taps his foot. It looks cartoonish; a monster lost in thought.

Burn the relays? But – no. We'd still risk these ugly buggers on our back.

What, then?

Haven't got time to fanny about is what. I still have to grab the box you brought in here. And the pick-up window is only three minutes –

What are you talking about?

You'll see.

I can't leave him. We can't do that to him. I've never been more fucking sure about anything.

Might have to, pal. Miss the pick-up, the world comes down on this building with us inside.

Let it. Let the lot swallow me up.

Get a grip. Air in your lungs yet.

The boy mewls.

I can't stay here, Brian says. Oh God, Noah, what have you done? What's happened to you?

We have to leave him.

Brian stares at the boy. Brian stares into the boy.

The boy smiles, his wet chin and bruised neck. His dark-stained trousers and the sparse fluff across his top lip.

Brian touches the plastiglass casing. He draws a heart with fingertip grease. He says, We'll come back for you.

And he wonders if the boy thinks he's going for a slash. If he'll wait with that same gormless grin on him; the same empty eyes; whether the spit on his chin will crust and yellow.

It gets too much, thinking that way. Brian can feel his stomach rise, a panic, the shock of loss. It's the guilt of apathy, striking sooner than later. The guilt of hindsight, projected back from some grimmer, greyer future.

I promise, he says. I'll come back for you.

Sirens outside cut the town hall down the middle.

Not got long, Noah says. He has the copper on reception by the hair, his other hand on the crotch. Brian watches from his dead-tree throne.

Where's the box?

The copper doesn't know. Came off curfew duty about the time this fancy dress horror show gripped his neck and weighed him in. New to consciousness, the copper has the glazed eyes of anyone who'll do anything to escape a bad situation.

You must have storage, Brian says.

Noah looks over his shoulder. He says, Shurrup, lad. Enough good-cop from you.

You can see the copper is twisting and writhing. He's saying: I can't – I can't –

So Noah strokes the man's cheek and smiles. He says, Hush up, sweetheart.

Noah exposes his own empty gums, the black pits where now-dead teeth lived. The gaps between the cord of his tattered cheek muscles.

Copper here fumbles his keys, his hands trembling, his wrists gone slack. And Noah kisses the copper fully on the mouth. Forces the protestations back down his throat just as the flies fill the room.

Tracking his eyes as they roll away, Brian sees the copper wilt.

You really can, Noah says.

Brian takes the box on his lap.

You're a monster, he tells his old buddy-old pal. Look at you. A beast.

It's dark out. It's spitting too. Brian doesn't know the time.

With Noah, he watches the storm of flies rise into the black.

There are new smells – burnt plastic and diesel fumes. The cobalt clouds have an orange fringe; the city burning up around them. Sirens glitching out on the hard wind. Running battles fought over long days. From here, the town hall roof, they can see some of the camps and barricades. Roadblocks and dead zones, bodies and walls turned to twaddle. Neon pictures and building wraps flicker wildly, others faltering to pale shapes and dull sheen. Some of the famous ones are plain dead altogether.

Above them, a sentinel for their city, the town hall's clock tower. Its clocks stopped at the moment those backpacks brought down the Beetham. Below, the statue of John Bright, spray-painted glowstick green.

Brian wonders if his house is burning in the firestorm, too.

The odd crack of a gun sounds out, half-arsed somehow. And then there's a volley sent back in return – tracer rounds every few. It feels like capitulation. They've all got themselves in this mess, realised too late the effort needed to get back out. Everyone gunning scared. Hoping that if they miss, they won't have to clean anything up.

Brian chews his fingers, runs his hands across the flank of the box. Noah, whatever he is, looks out on the war.

Noah says something Brian doesn't catch.

Say again?

I said, You ever miss them straplines and slogans. Bit of wit on our walls. Because I do.

Pack it in, Noah. The hell d'you mean?

These pictures and fancy lights. When I were a lad. He stops, laughs at the cliché – or maybe at how old he's caught himself. He tries again: When I started out climbing ladders, ropes, draping this stuff across our city, there were words. Don't mean just big names like now – I mean messages. Slogans and that. All this, or how it was till the other day, it's like we've regressed, isn't it? They're all bloody pictures and big-budget names. Like we're kids who can't understand owt more than a pair of baps waved in our faces. Used to be agencies and writers and concepts. Wit. That's what I mean.

I don't really care, says Brian. Don't notice any of it.

You think that. But you'd reach for these brands. Burnt into your head, mate. Connect a picture, connect an idea, reinforce the idea with a picture – it's clever, aye, but stone me it's cynical.

Can't remember the last time I bought anything.

You nearly bought it full stop in there.

I've got bloody gills, Noah.

Noah stretches out and tents up his wings – has to lean back against the wind so as to not topple off the roof. Slowly, purposefully, he pulls a strip of skin from his stomach – a ruler's width, fully five inches – and balls it up between his hands. Then, he kicks it skyways.

We win some, and we lose some, he says. You remember my story of the ponies on Ascension Island, don't you? We're just adapting pal. The two of us. We looked at the bottom of that box and saw something we liked. And look at you. You are glorious. You are a swan now.

How long do we wait? asks Brian.

Long as we need to, chum.

Who're we waiting for?

Cavalry. Just like your old films.

They look out on the city as it burns. Sirens and paper on the air.

Maybe this'll change things, Noah says. Like when they burn the heather up on the moors. Looks rotten now, like, but –

Didn't change owt last time, did it?

Maybe last time the fire got to all the peat and seeds underneath.

Hardly a moor-keeper to look out for that.

Noah sighs.

Well, give us a fag then.

But an image, a new memory of smell, makes Brian retch.

Turns out the cavalry is Tariq. Four floors down with a torch flashing up in morse code.

How does he know we're here? Brian asks, as close to the edge as he can manage.

That one's a complicated question, says Noah.

Brian can't work out why Noah keeps looking over the edge.

Come on, Brian says, nodding back inside. Stairwell's back here. I'll go on my arse if you grab my chair. Noah? What's the matter with you? Look like you're going to jump.

Noah laughs.

Course I bloody am. And you'll be in my arms, sunshine.

Brian rolls up. Brian peers out on to the sheer face, the gothic protrusions. He feels gravity's pull against the push of sense; thinks about the leap of faith they'd need to miss the whole lot on the way down. Brian gets an idea of impaling themselves – two fast bodies dashed over hard, old stone. Hitting the split pavement flags and splitting themselves. Slashed and separated out by the sharpline ringing the building.

Where's all this going to end? he asks.

Noah puts a clawed hand to Brian's shoulder.

It's in hand. All in hand.

Heard that before, haven't we?

You'll see.

Noah scoops Brian from his chair and secures Colin's box to a wrist. He steps, eyes shut, throwing his wings out and into battle formation. He touches a finger to Brian's chest. A little left, centred on the heart.

He whispers, It beats climbing them. For all my years – all my sins climbing this city for Harry with some big cunt's name rolled up in a tube on my back. This, this even beats what I did on the Beetham that day, Bri.

210

Climbing the bastard with nowt but the balls between my legs.

This.

Noah dives off the building and Brian's with him and Brian feels straighter than he has in years.

Laughing and falling – fast.

Superman, Brian breathes.

Noah's powdered wings are spread fully wide, the wind whistling across their edges like a child trying to play grass.

The sides of all these buildings flaring electric blue.

Brian, carried like a newly-wed in Noah's flaking arms, has dead-heart dread. At three metres and closing, he can see how Tariq got the pig parked so close. Brian sees it through the sideglass – the lapels and collar. The shoulder stripes on him. The bloody riot helmet on the passenger seat.

Brian half-gasps, a breath cut short as the half-track's whopping engine fires up. The fat exhaust kicks up a plume of ash, the whole thing tipping, rocking on its axles. Noah carries Brian through a half-second of hesitance.

And Tariq, Tariq winds down the window and screams: Get thee the fuck in, lads.

With the door open, Noah more-or-less throws Brian onto the bench seat.

Blues on, sirens on, the closed loop radio screaming gabbled static.

Not you, goes Brian to Tariq. Tell me it's a joke.

You get your good eggs and your bad eggs, Tariq says. I would've told you sooner.

A bloody plod. All this time –

That's how you got round the curfew.

Did you fit me up for that? For them in there?

Not sectioned to Manchester, brother. We –

What you mean? Undercover?

Sort of, aye. MET sent me. Anti-terrorism and that. I'm the wrong shade of white for owt else worth doing.

Christ above. Those bastards are worse than ours. Government?

It's a contract. Can't say owt else.

Tariq's looking in his mirror. Three days of stubble and he's halfway to Ghandi.

You told him what's going on, Noah?

Noah shakes his head. The flaps of his cheeks peel away and stick themselves back to mucus.

Brian asks what's going on. He says, You as well?

Noah shakes his head again.

Don't fret on, will you? You're always bloody fretting on. You think a serving officer's going to get down here knowing what a murderous swine I've been all day, and then drop you back in it? Bigger fish, son.

Well how else would you know I was there?

Brian eyes Colin's box. Noah's tapping it with a single talon of bone – the flesh gone entirely from the forefinger.

Nobody says anything.

Get him warm, says Tariq. That grey face says he's not long from shock.

Noah remembers that part. Noah leans down and pulls out a blanket, a flask. He passes a pair of sugar cubes. He unscrews the flask lid and takes a sniff. A pearl of drool comes free from his chin.

Milk and honey, our kid, he says. And here, he adds, passing him a pair of sugar cubes. Get these down you an' all.

Brian can't get the wrapper off fast enough. The edges

of the cubes hurt his gums; he sucks hard, chews, has trouble swallowing the paste.

Noah nods approvingly. His ruined face half-masked by a wing. He pats the blanket on the seat between them.

I can tuck you up. Hold you tight.

Brian grabs it. He weakly flops about, cocooning himself in the blanket. Wouldn't want to guess what'll hatch out of this –

And Brian swigs at the thermos. Takes the heat and the sweetness to heart.

He closes his eyes.

The half-track, the pig, bumbles on through the firestorm.

19.

They see one of these pigs with the doors hanging off its back. Rum buggers had got a pipebomb in there. They see a pram filled with bottles, virgin-white rags in their collars, yet to be lit.

They see children bouncing on a holoboard they've pulled off a pawn shop. So many shutters ripped off their frames, bent out like the bristles of old toothbrushes. Tendrils of tear gas, the ghost of cotton smog. The war cries.

And they all squirm when Tariq's pig runs a barricade and comes away with a bloodied protestor on its nose. Through double-skin glass, he's shouting all sorts. Tariq swings left but adrenaline makes the bloke too sticky. Dead keen, this one, someone says. So Tariq brakes till he's gone under the front wing, and they hope the half-track's ground clearance was enough because you sure as hell can't see out the back owing to the ash and dust and muck on the windows.

Nobody talks. Nobody says anything as they swing by a mob setting fires; scattering as the diesel engine sounds out. Bodies line the road, statue-hard, exactly as they've fallen. Near them, a woman crawls along the pavement, one side of her head pulped, her cheeks puffy. She's calling a name – David, David, it sounds like. But they have to drive on because sticks and stones are clattering off the panels.

One brick digs itself into the first pane of the windscreen. It has a red corner, a clump of hair. Something pink and fatty on it. Then a flash of something bright zaps across the bonnet – fumes alight, turning blue, and gone again. Masonry rolls off the buildings; endless bits of paper and insulation riding air as though caught in the fetch of a wave.

Another corner, another scene. An old man sitting on the kerb with a young boy across his lap. His white shirt reddening against the boy's belly. Desperate coppers at the top of the road, sprinting towards the half-track and waving for it to stop. Beyond them, a gang with burning road barriers legging it after them.

The half-track doesn't stop. Two people bounce off, ploughed to the sides. The gang are flanking the half-track, black, brown, white faces through the windows. A shotgun flares, a dull pop –

The broken lines and broken helmets.

We've lost the streets, says Tariq.

No, says, Brian, still caught between his dreams and these nightmares. We've won them back.

Further on, farther away, Brian asks how they found him. Mainly because Colin's box already says enough about why they wanted to.

Brian says, Fluke or chance or – pointing at Tariq – was it this bastard here, his pals back in there?

Shifting his gaze to the mirror, Tariq coughs. Noah takes some kind of cue.

Do you trust me?

That was Noah.

Don't know any more, says Brian.

Young lass, weren't she Tariq? says Noah. Twenty or twenty-one. Dead bonny, too – you would, and you'd be rude not to. But she saunters up not too long back, can't for life of me remember where, and says she knows me. She knows you an' all. Knows about everything.

Brian's skin shifts on its frame.

So I say, I say, What are you, some kind of witch? And she goes, No darling, I'm an empress.

Juliet? says Brian. That her name?

Noah shakes his head. She tells me she's called Constance.

Brian stares at him.

Dark hair? You're sure that were her name?

Oh aye. You wouldn't want to miss her. And she goes, Your friend Brian's a very silly billy –

Brian throws the flask, sends white globes spinning across the bench seat, the roof lining.

But how? he screams. She's a little girl!

Once was, Noah says.

Then she's a frigging witch as well, whispers Brian.

No, says Noah sadly.

She's definitely an empress.

The pig rolls on. The pig rolls through the broken streets, the burning city. The slate tide washing blood to the grids.

The twin-smell of diesel and sweat; the burning paper and the bodies.

Brian, Noah says. His eyes seem so sad. It's sorted, now.

Brian nods. His red-rimmed eyes, his face the colour of t-shirts you've washed too many times.

Noah has a syringe. Noah has a firm grip and a vein worth aiming for.

This won't hurt –

216

20.

It didn't hurt.

But the sunshine does. The hangover.

On first glance, there's sunshine, a piercing view. Then green hills, glinting glass bodies of a city wrapped around itself in glee. The steaming towers of industry. Wind turbines, stretched across the hills like an upscaled Normandy cemetery, all spinning hard for the better good.

Here's a relic of something they all knew, only fresh and tall and proud and bright. Together they stand on its blunt tip, its box-flat roof. The snub-nose spire of an icon they lost. No fire, no guns –

There's a digital sign board running the top panel. It says, IT'S A BRIGHT OUTLOOK IN THE NORTH.

All at once, in tides:

He's standing on the Beetham tower, but before the fall. Standing with hands under his armpits, his tail just touching the floor.

Brian gets motion sickness, then. A kind of vertigo. He leans and spews, mainly at the realisation. It's all fluid. It's all black. A filthy by-product of a very real shock. Still black, still rotten –

How? He says. How?

But that's the thing with rhetorical questions. Nobody needs to answer.

Brian looks down and takes in the stainless steel pip-

217

ing that encases his pelvis. The stoppers, the rubber feet. Servo motors at knee-height, coils and springs and pneumatic rams.

How-do, says a woman.

In front of him, in deck chairs, Juliet and her daughter, Constance. To their side, a purple Transit van, side door open.

Noah. Tariq. And Colin.

Brian says, Am I dead? He must say it earnestly, too – they all pull a smile.

No, says Juliet. Not dead.

Asleep?

No, not that either. But you can move. Try it.

Brian, his throat burning, inches forward. The frame around him gives, hisses, takes his weight and interprets his intent. As it compensates, he bobs up, advancing slowly. He winces. He's still very weak. Very unsteady. He can feel bruises in places you've never had a bruise.

It'll take you a bit of time to get used to it, Juliet says. But here, you have plenty of that.

Where am I?

Manchester.

How is this Manchester?

Another Manchester. We brought you here.

We? How?

Me, Colin, Constance. In the van.

Colin's not –

No, not this one.

Where's my box?

Juliet smiles. She points to the van.

Come on, now. It's not yours.

Brian, dazed, simply nods.

And he – Colin – isn't dead?

Not this version of him, no.

You mean you keep copies?

Sort of. Anything else?

Are you from space?

No. But another place. You're our neighbours by five. This, this Manchester, this is the middle-point between yours and ours.

So how do you get around?

Juliet points to the van again.

Brian puts his face in his hands.

It's okay, says Juliet. You aren't expected to take it all in.

But my box –

The box was a trap. Bait. Whatever you want to call it. And not for you, either. Ian's supposed to open it at his event, isn't he. In that quiet room afterwards. You saw it, didn't you?

I was there.

We were intervening. The why doesn't bear mentioning.

But you'd approached me before then. The house. The shoe-shop.

Juliet nods. Well, I once asked if you believed in fate, she says.

Aye.

Well how d'you think we had this frame ready for you?

I don't follow.

With some degree of variance, you were going to end up here.

You can see the future?

Enough as needs seeing. The past as well. When we realised you got involved it had to be checked out.

Then you are a witch.

No more than you're a monster, she tells him.

You let me suffer. You let this box affect me –

Said this before as well, haven't I. It's not all about you. But the box. The box and the riots. The police station –

I'm not sorry, says Juliet. You had plenty of opportunity. Would've been fine if you pair hadn't stuck your noses so far in. And look – what's in that box is part of something wider we still don't fully understand. A by-product of slipping between worlds. Used properly, it seems to make its own distortions there and then. Used improperly . . . well of course we have to clean up the mess.

I don't follow. If you knew I'd take the box, you knew what would happen. You didn't have to let it.

Brian. We can't just change things without serious consideration and planning. One small thing can be so enormous a day, a week, a decade later. So we planned on-the-fly – a way to get the box that wouldn't mean altering too much, too suddenly. I can't account for your will, your weakness. Nor Noah's. Nobody can. Plus time is so flexible when you know how.

People are dead. Diane –

I know. And it's . . . she . . . that was regrettable.

You don't know anything. You're saying you could've stopped that. You could've stepped in sooner. You let me think Noah was too.

I've had to grow a hard heart, Brian. We tried. We tried before Ian got to you. Before Noah could change. We watched to understand you – but first we had to find you. The right you – not a you from one slip, two slips across. Not a you on another path; some other string. So when I came to your house, I'd got the right person. But by the time you'd got the box, I'd been thrown off by a you who made a different decision altogether. Do you see?

Then why Ian at all?

220

We're investigating him. His future interests. On the course he was taking, he'd become a big problem for a lot of people. Don't mince my words, Brian. With that man, genocide wouldn't be far off.

Brian looks away.

We can't be too careful about what's changed and what isn't, Juliet says. The box was intended to help Ian . . . undo himself.

I see, says Brian. But all this and you don't even say who you work for.

That's because we work for everybody. You, me and everybody.

The Wilbers say that and all, says Brian. Ian's lot – the nationalists, skin-heads – they all say that. The council minders and the rich beggars in their towers. Everybody works for everybody. And everybody works for themselves.

And you then. Who do you work for? What have you done for somebody, anybody?

I left a boy to rot.

You got Constance working for it, too, have you? He gestures at Tariq and Noah. Because she came for them two, didn't she?

What's that got to do with anything? A distant her, yes. But like I say, it gets complicated. Logistics get tight. You make do. You have to fill in the holes any way you can. As and when they happen. Constance – the older Constance – had favours to pay off. It was necessary –

Is this terminal? What I'm turning into? This cancer you've put through my bones?

Brian looks over at Noah. The audience is rapt. His condition the way it is. He already knows it's terminal. The vomit was sludge, inky. Its foul taste didn't suggest something that might improve.

Probably, yes.

Then – and he pauses – I'd like to take our box back to Ian myself. It'll be my trident. See what he finds in the bottom of himself.

They're pretending like it's happy families on the roof. On top of this ghost that in Brian's world turns to a pillar of light by night.

Brian walks circles in his new frame, his servo-powered zimmer. How convenient all that other crap was – the chairs he lost during earlier nights. Seems a hollow victory – not least when you consider how Brian's thoughts are tangled around revenge and redemption. His old buddy, his old pal, Noah, sitting there with hunched wings, obscene, playing rock paper scissors with a giddy little Constance. Colin, bearded skinny Colin, who died in another world and didn't in this one. Tariq, the copper, an arrow-straight, upstanding copper. Juliet. This witch in a vest. Constance. The empress on her forty-seven-storey throne. And Brian, standing, walking, all on his own.

Yet in some ways, Brian does not want for anything. Not weed, not beer, not cigarettes nor coke. Maybe a bath. A salt-water soak. But mostly, Ian's head on a platter; hands tight round his throat.

Now, Colin asks Brian for a quiet word. He motions to the van. A small favour, he says. To help us understand what's going on.

Across the roof, Colin can tell Brian is anxious about the van. So Colin gives him the facts. It has jets. Some kind of fission device to power it. Gravity manipulators and other fancy words. He says, Don't look so upset. Where I'm from, we all use these.

Brian listens. They walk on a little more. Or Brian does his best to.

222

Brian asks, Did you know the you on that stage?

Colin smiles.

He came over from fifteen across, I think. Truthfully, I don't tend to deal with myselves. Freaks you out. Juliet manages HR.

So you've got all these versions of you selling ideas across the gaps?

Colin nods. Smiles.

The ones we could convince, I suppose. It's a war, where we're from, he says. Have to fund these things, don't you?

Brian squeezes his nose.

And there are more? Doing what you're doing?

A fair few in the group now, aye. Some drift – lapse. Kind of hard to keep track when there are so many versions of everyone. Plus a few found better lives through the slip, and didn't bother coming back. Hard to blame them really. So much to see, isn't there. The little differences between one world and the very next. But likewise you can go on forever, till one day something makes you pause –

Not much worth finding in ours, then, says Brian.

Colin unzips a holdall. Inside there's a flask, some kind of autoclave.

The politics are interesting, he says, looking at Brian's tail. And the box . . . the biology is absolutely fascinating –

Brian grunts.

The politics.

Sure the politics. Everyone seems to want the old world, the old way, but can't agree on the right road back there. And the more you look at that problem, the more you can't see any way round it. I don't understand who's protesting for what in that country of yours. It's like it's just something for people to do.

And what if it is? says Brian. Nowt else, is there.

Probably best it burns. Here, let me just clean up –

Colin squirts the air from a syringe. He swabs Brian's forearm. He says, Really appreciate this. It'll help us understand.

The needle slides home. The syringe body fills with a navy blue. Colin's eyes go wide. He taps the plastic; holds it against the light.

Well look at that, goes Colin. You're royalty.

If the box posed a question about what he was for, Brian knows the answer now. Because the enormity of all this doesn't really wash. The dizzying image of clean Manchester; Salford, there again; the low clouds putting a hat on the Pennines. Because it's hollow. The kind of dream a full bladder will pull you away from.

There's a bloating woman hanging over his staircase. There's a toothless boy in the town hall –

On the roof, the highest point in this warped, fairytale version of Manchester, Juliet clears her throat. She asks something –

The breeze catches an edge of the Beetham and drags out a note. Brian remembers the songs of this tower. In strong winds, the whole city could hear it hum.

Juliet repeats the question. She says, And it's safer here. This walker frame is yours to keep. You'll have the support you want, the care you need –

Brian says, No.

Brian says, You have to take me back.

And with that, his heart stops cracking.

Because you love your country in spite of your country.

Brian and Noah look out to Werneth Low from a tower that never fell. That was never bombed. Between them

– between the point of the hill and the building's base on Deansgate – lie ten miles of buildings and roads and parks and homes. Railways and bus routes. Corner shops and pub dinners –

Like the olden days, says Brian. Pretty plain without your adverts and logos, mind. Hardly a tube of neon, is there.

Not my cup of tea, says Noah. Wouldn't be, though. Didn't decorate any of it, did I?

Brian shakes his head.

So it's a fresh palette. It's a canvas for my best yet. An outrageous bloody playground for me to colour in. Starting with a pair of tits and a grin –

Brian laughs. The walking suit shivers around him.

And they aren't a bad bunch, you know, says Noah. Juliet got me out of a hole, too.

Well, I can't thank any of you, says Brian.

That's all right, son. I don't want that.

Aye, but I want to. But your promises. Your lies –

Well if you're really leaving, I'll at least come for the ride.

I want that kid out of the town hall. You can come as far as there. It'll be one last thing. Bring him here. Make sure he's looked after. Besides, them things on your back make for a better Superman.

Noah smiles.

OK, he says, hand on heart. One last thing.

21.

Juliet brings them home in the Transit. She has directions and maps, a semi-auto pistol nestled in her lap.

It works like this, the slip. You're loaded in. You sit damn still. You strap up, shut up. Say your byes and keep that chin up.

Brian closes his eyes on green fields and silver glass –

The van slips. Explodes across every colour of the rainbow. He opens his eyes. They roll about in the swill of black limbo. Brian sees galaxies and belts of frozen stone, majestic comets off the stern that sail over, so close you can see colours, fine crystal, the treasures inside. It's some private vision of heaven, without worldly things at all. His hands look funny, like mousse, a froth of pink on liquid bones. They float on a sea of absolutes. Brian closes his eyes. Brian hears his heartbeat swell –

Opens his eyes to fire and hell.

Juliet dials something in. Unbuckles and turns fully round.

Welcome home, children. You might feel nauseous – can't account for turbulence.

Turbulence? asks Noah. Where are we?

Same place. Just forty-seven floors over your memorial lamp.

Stripes of orange mark the grid of Manchester's plan. Juliet wrestles with yaw to position the Transit, swearing mildly.

Okay, she says. You're good. You're set. Town hall's a straight stone down.

The whispers in the back: And you definitely want this?

That was Noah.

Brian nods. He smoothes the stubble on his head.

You know they're really bloody interested in your changes.

Stands to reason, doesn't it, goes Brian. To look at me. But yours too, Moth-boy. You can stay in touch.

I look a damn sight worse than you, pal.

You're not wrong.

What's going to happen to the shoe shop? asks Brian.

Only bricks and mortar.

Got an answer for everything, haven't you?

The van doors open. Noah puts a wet finger out into the air, checking the wind.

Of course, he says.

I won't miss you, Brian tells him.

Noah drops, blowing a kiss.

Already the tarmac has gone to weeds. They've crossed the dusk yards; the shapes of the Pennines sharpening ahead. Manchester is a smashed lava lamp in the Transit's mirrors, an orange-yellow smudge bleeding into the cloud above it.

It looks gorgeous, Brian's city in flames.

Juliet swings right at Flouch roundabout.

She doesn't say a word.

22.

Brian means to accept himself.

The cloaksuit he asked for ghosts his hands, but not the noise. The walker frame, for all its precision-machined parts, for all its greased bearings, still clatters like a maraca tossed down a well. He throws the bolt cutters under a bush. He pockets the foot of sharpline he's taken out of the fence.

Birds scatter and chatter the second he pushes through the shrubbery and onto the back lawn.

On the lawn and panting, sweating. The smell of fish and the smell of dew.

After every sharp movement, pause for thought.

He counts three lads on patrol. Same style Salford boys they met first time round. He locks the legs, these skinny legs on either side.

If you're on open ground, go forward a metre, wait a minute –

The bandstand is just over there, its roof the shape of a deflated church bell. In the house, Ian's fortress, all the lights are off. This early in the morning, there's a dull sheen to everything; that cold filter that casts your skin in grey.

If someone spots you, remember they haven't. They can't see you. And if they think they've seen you, keep still: they'll soon think they haven't.

Brian ambles, totters, wheezing through exertion. It's absolutely a shuffle, this – he isn't quite used to the

228

gyros, the rolling motion, the feeling he's always at the edge of his balance. That's because there's a pivot at his waist, and his fused feet form the central leg. He's a kind of biomechanical tripod, now, so when he's got his meat forward, the two steel legs compensate behind. It makes for slow progress.

But it's progress.

Under the bandstand, pondside, Brian steadies himself in the walker unit. He can smell the water now, can see the carp as they rise, scatter and regroup. A spirograph of orange and silver, black and mottled brown.

Brian pours a lot of salt into the koi pond. He hears the filter grind, or thinks he does.

At first the fish thrash and scatter – working faster than any temperature would make them. They dart here, rolling on themselves, crashing in blind panic.

He watches the fish working harder.

He watches and pours the salt.

He keeps pouring. The fish rise to the surface, rolling about on their sides, their gills turned a deep red.

He unstraps himself. Turns off the cloaksuit and has a word with the buckles. He unwraps his tail. He runs a hand around it, up and down. The scales here have turned to rainbow – pearlescent golds and purples caught in this scant light. He's wearing nothing for a top, and his chest hair has long since come off.

The fin on his back, the wound that's flowered, unfurls as he leans away from the walking frame.

Naked, he slips into the water – as elegant as he's never been. He parts the dead and dying fish gently; brothers now, sisters now, family from another time. A shame they were not sharks, marine flounder, some other kind, else he'd have swam here with them. His tail reacts to the

229

salt, gently rippling as the powerful muscles adjust.

He raises his arms so that his shoulders crest the water line. He feels his gills begin to suck.

He dips his head; breathes it in.

A last breath, more out of tradition than necessity, and he's under. Maritime man, with his gold-gilded tail.

To wait.

Through the floating fish, Brian sees the shimmer-silhouette above. The length of the man, warped, distorted by the surface, and outlined by the dawn light. He sees the frozen limbs of a baffled man, and it comforts him. He hears shouts, muffled, and lets a single bubble go with a grin. In his hands, that foot length of sharpline.

He pulls it taut.

Good strong wire for great, noble deeds. Because this is the final myth. It's what a mermaid is for; what a mermaid does. He is the siren on the masthead, the fate of drowning lovers, the figure by the rockpools.

If his mother could see –

Ian leans in and bulges large; leans in to pick out his dead children from the pond. His head shimmies across the pond's skin. The surface tension breaks.

And Brian, clever Brian, rises to meet him. Not as half a man, but fully a mermaid.